further interpretations
of real-life events

ALSO BY KEVIN MOFFETT

Permanent Visitors

further interpretations
of real-life events

stories

KEVIN MOFFETT

HARPER PERENNIAL

NEW YORK • LONDON • TORONTO • SYDNEY • NEW DELHI • AUCKLAND

HARPER ● PERENNIAL

HarperCollins books may be purchased for educational, business, or sales
promotional use. For information, please write: Special Markets Department,
HarperCollins Publishers, 10 East 53rd Street, New York, NY 10022.

Grateful acknowledgment is made to the publications in which many of these
stories originally appeared (some in slightly different versions).

"Further Interpretations of Real-Life Events" in *McSweeney's*; reprinted in
The Best American Short Stories 2010

"Buzzers" in *Ecotone*

"In the Pines" in *Harvard Review*

"First Marriage" in *Land-Grant College Review*; reprinted in
New Stories from the South: The Year's Best 2008

"Lugo in Normal Time" in *McSweeney's*

"English Made Easy" in *American Short Fiction*

"The Big Finish" in *FiveChapters*

"One Dog Year" in *Tin House*; reprinted in *The Best American Short Stories 2009*

FIRST EDITION

Designed by Jennifer Daddio / Bookmark Design & Media Inc.

Library of Congress Cataloging-in-Publication Data

Moffett, Kevin.
Further interpretations of real-life events : stories / Kevin Moffett. — 1st ed.
p. cm.
ISBN 978-0-06-206922-1
I. Title.

PS3613.O365F87   2011
813'.6—dc22
2011012898

11 12 13 14 15   OV/RRD   10 9 8 7 6 5 4 3 2 1

for ellis

contents

further interpretations
of real-life events

After my father retired, he began writing trueish
stories about fathers and sons. He had tried scuba
diving, had tried being a dreams enthusiast, and
now he'd come around to this. I was skeptical. I'd
been writing my own trueish stories about fathers
and sons for years, stories that weren't perfect, of
course, but they were mine. Some were published
in literary journals, and I'd even received a fan letter

from Helen in Vermont, who liked the part in one of my stories where the father made the boy scratch his stepmom's back. Helen in Vermont said she found the story "enjoyable" but kind of "depressing."

The scene with the stepmom was an interpretation of an actual event. When I was ten years old, my mother died. My father and I lived alone for five years, until he married Lara, a kind woman with a big laugh. He met her at a dreams conference. I liked her well enough in real life but not in the story. In the story, "End of Summer," I resented Lara (changed to "Laura") for marrying my father so soon after my mother died (changed to five months).

"You used to scratch your ma's back all the time," my father says in the final scene. "Why don't you ever scratch Laura's?"

Laura sits next to me, shucking peas into a bucket. The pressure builds. "If you don't scratch Laura's back," my father says, "you can forget Christmas!"

So I scratch her back. It sounds silly now, but by the end of the story, Christmas stands in for other things. It isn't just Christmas anymore.

The scene was inspired by the time my father and Lara went to Mexico City (while I was marauded by bullies and blackflies at oboe camp) and brought me home a souvenir. A tin handicraft? you guess. A selection of cactus-fruit candy? No. A wooden back-scratcher with extended handle for maximum self-gratification. What's worse, *Te quiero* was embossed on the handle. Which I translated at the time to mean "I love me." (I was off by one word.)

"Try it," my father said. His tan had a yolky tint and he wore a T-shirt with PROPERTY OF MEXICO on the back. It was the sort of shirt you could find anywhere.

I hiked my arm over my head and raked the back-scratcher north and south along my vertebrae. "Works," I said.

"He spent all week searching for something for you," Lara said. "He even tried to haggle at the *mercado*. It was cute."

"There isn't much for a boy like you in Mexico," my father said. "The man who sold me the back-scratcher, though, told me a story. All the men who left to fight during the revolution took their wives with them. They wanted to remember more . . ."

I couldn't listen. I tried to, I pretended to, nodding and going *hmm* when he said *Pancho Villa*, and *wow* when he said *gunfire*, and then *some story* when it was over. I excused myself, sprinted upstairs to my bedroom, slammed my door, and snapped that sorry back-scratcher over my knee like kindling.

A boy like me!

•

You'll never earn a living writing stories, not if you're any good at it. My mentor Harry Hodgett told me that. I must've been doing something right, because I had yet to receive a dime for my work. I day-labored at the community college teaching Prep Writing, a class for students without the necessary skills for Beginning Writing. I also taught Prep Prep Writing, for those without the skills for Prep Writing. Imagine the most abject students on earth, kids who, when you ask them to name a verb, stare like you just asked them to cluck out a polka with armpit farts.

Literary journals paid with contributors' copies and subscriptions, which was nice, because when your story was published, you at least knew that everyone else in the issue would read your work. (Though, truth be told, I never did.) This was how I came to receive the autumn issue of *Vesper*—I'd been published in the spring issue. It sat on my coffee table until a few days after its arrival, when I returned home to find Carrie on my living-room sofa, reading it. "Shh," she said.

I'd just come back from teaching, dispirited as usual after Shandra Jones in Prep Prep Writing told a classmate to "eat my drippins." A bomb I defused with clumsy silence, comma time!, early dismissal.

"I didn't say anything," I said.

"Shh," she said again.

An aside: I'd like to have kept Carrie out of this, because I haven't figured out how to write about her. She's tall with short brown hair and brown eyes and she wears clothes and—see? I could be describing anybody. Carrie's lovely, her face is a nest for my dreams. You need distance from your subject matter. You need to approach it with the icy, lucid eye of a surgeon. I also can't write about my mother. Whenever I try, I feel like I'm attempting kidney transplants with a can opener and a handful of rubber bands.

"Amazing," she said, closing the journal. "Sad and honest and free of easy meanness. It's like the story was unfolding as I read it. That bit in the motel: wow. How come you never showed me this? It's a breakthrough."

She stood and hugged me. She smelled like bath beads. I was jealous of the person, whoever it was, who had effected this reaction in her: Carrie, whom I met in Hodgett's class, usually read my stories with barely concealed impatience.

"Breakthrough, huh?" I said casually (desperately). "Who wrote it?"

She leaned in and kissed me. "You did."

I picked up the journal to make sure it wasn't the spring issue, which featured "The Longest Day of the Year," part two of my summer trilogy. It's about a boy and his father (I know, I know) driving home, arguing about the record player the father refuses to buy the boy, even though the boy totally needs it since his current one ruined two of his Yes albums, including the impossible-to-find *Time and a Word*, and—*boom*—they hit a deer. The stakes suddenly shift.

I turned to the contributors' notes. FREDERICK MOXLEY *is a retired statistics professor living in Vero Beach, Florida. In his spare time he is a dreams enthusiast. This is his first published story.*

"My dad!" I screamed. "He stole my name and turned me into a dreams enthusiast!"

"Your *dad* wrote this?"

"And turned me into a goddamn dreams enthusiast! Everyone'll think I've gone soft and stupid!"

"I don't think anyone really reads this journal," Carrie said. "No offense. And isn't he Frederick Moxley, too?"

"Fred! He goes by Fred. I go by Frederick. Ever since third grade, when there were two Freds in my class." I flipped the pages, found the story, "Mile Zero," and read the first sentence: *As a boy, I always dreamed of flight.* That makes two of us, I thought. To the circus, to Tibet, to live with a nice family of Moonies. I felt tendrils of bile beanstalking up my throat. "What's he trying to do?"

"Read it," Carrie said. "I think he makes it clear what he's trying to do."

If the story was awful, I could easily have endured it, I realize now. I could've called him and said if he insists on writing elderly squibs, please just use a pseudonym. Let the Moxley interested in truth and beauty, etc., publish under his real name. But the story wasn't awful. Not by a long shot. Yes, it broke two of Hodgett's six laws of story-writing (Never dramatize a dream; Never use more than one exclamation point per story), but he'd managed some genuine insight. Also he fictionalized real-life events in surprising ways. I recognized one particular detail from after Mom died. We moved the following year, because my father never liked our house's floor plan. That's what I'd thought, at least. Too cramped, he always said; wherever you turned, a wall or closet blocked your path. In the story, though, the characters move because the father can't disassociate the house from his wife. Her presence is everywhere: in the bedroom, the bathroom, in the silverware pattern, the flowering jacaranda in the backyard.

She used to trim purple blooms from the tree and scatter them around the house, on bookshelves, on the dining-room table, he wrote. *It seemed a perfectly attuned response to the natural world, a way of inviting the outside inside.*

I remembered those blooms. I remembered how the house smelled with her in it, though I couldn't name the smell. I recalled her presence, vast ineffable thing.

I finished reading in the bath. I was no longer angry. I was a little jealous. Mostly I was sad. The story, which showed father and son failing to connect again and again, ends in a motel room in Big Pine Key (we used to go there in December), the father watching a cop show on TV while the boy sleeps. He's having a bad dream, the father can tell by the way his face winces and frowns. The father lies down next to him, hesitant to wake him up, and tries to imagine what he's dreaming about.

Don't wake up, the father tells him. *Nothing in your sleep can hurt you.*

The boy was probably dreaming of a helicopter losing altitude. It was a recurring nightmare of mine after Mom died.

I'd be cutting through the sky, past my house, past the hospital, when suddenly the control panel starts beeping and the helicopter spins down, down. My body fills with air as I yank the joystick. The noise is the worst. Like a monster oncoming bee. My head buzzes long after I wake up, shower, and sit down to breakfast. My father, who's just begun enthusing about dreams, a hobby that even then I found ridiculous, asks what I dreamed about.

"Well," I say between spoonfuls of cereal. "I'm in a blue—no, no, a golden suit. And all of a sudden I'm swimming in an enormous fishbowl in a pet store filled with eager customers. And the thing is, they all look like you. The other thing is, I love it. I want to stay in the fishbowl forever. Any idea what that means?"

"Finish your breakfast," he says, eyes downcast.

I'd like to add a part where I say *just kidding*, then tell him my dream. He could decide it's about anxiety, or fear. Even better: he could just backhand me. I could walk around with a handprint on my face. It could go from red to purple to brownish blue, poetic-like. Instead, we sulked. It happened again and again, until mornings grew as joyless and choreographed as the interactions of people who worked among deafening machines.

In the bathroom, I dried myself off and wrapped a towel around my waist. I found Carrie in the kitchen eating oyster crackers. "So?" she said.

Her expression was so beseeching, such a lidless empty jug.

I tossed the journal onto the table. "Awful," I said. "Sentimental, boring. I don't know. Maybe I'm just biased against bad writing."

"And maybe," she said, "you're just jealous of good writing." She dusted crumbs from her blouse. "I know it's good, you know it's good. You aren't going anywhere till you admit that."

"And where am I trying to go?"

She regarded me with a look I recalled from Hodgett's class. Bemused amusement. The first day, while Hodgett asked each of us to name our favorite book, then explained why we were wrong, I was daydreaming about this girl in a white V-neck reading my work and timidly approaching me afterward to ask, *What did the father's broken watch represent?* and me saying *futility*, or *despair*, and then maybe kissing her. She turned out to be the toughest reader in class, far tougher than Hodgett, who was usually content to make vague pronouncements about *patterning* and *the octane of the epiphany*. Carrie was cold and smart and meticulous. She crawled inside your story with a flashlight and blew out all your candles. She said of one of my early pieces, "On what planet do people actually talk to each other like this?" And: "Does this character do anything but shuck peas?"

I knew she was right about my father's story. But I didn't want to talk about it anymore. So I unfastened my towel and let it drop to the floor. "Uh-oh," I said. "What do you think of this plot device?"

She looked at me, down, up, down. "We're not doing anything until you admit your father wrote a good story."

"*Good?* What's that even mean? Like, can it fetch and speak and sit?"

"Good," Carrie repeated. "It's executed as vigorously as it's conceived. It isn't false or pretentious. It doesn't jerk the reader around to no effect. It lives by its own logic. It's poignant without trying too hard."

I looked down at my naked torso. At some point during her litany, I seemed to have developed an erection. My penis looked all eager, as if it wanted to join the discussion, and unnecessary. "In that case," I said, "I guess he wrote one good story. Do I have to be happy about it?"

"Now I want you to call him and tell him how much you like it."

I picked up the towel, refastened it, and started toward the living room.

"I'm just joking," she said. "You can call him later."

Dejected, I followed Carrie to my room. She won, she always won. I didn't even feel like having sex anymore. My room smelled like the bottom of a pond, like a turtle's moistly rotting cavity. She lay on my bed, still talking about my father's story. "I love that little boy in the motel room," she said, kissing me, taking off her shirt. "I love how he's still frowning in his sleep."

•

I never called my father, though I told Carrie I did. I said I called and congratulated him. "What's his next project?" she asked. Project! As if he was a famous architect or something. I said he's considering a number of projects, each project more poignant-without-trying-too-hard than the project before it.

He phoned a week later. I was reading my students' paragraph essays, feeling my soul wither with each word. The paragraphs were in response to a prompt: "Where do you go to be alone?" All the students, except one, went to their room to be alone. The exception was Daryl Ellington, who went to his rom.

"You sound busy," my father said.

"Just getting some work done," I said.

We exchanged postcard versions of our last few weeks. I'm fine, Carrie's fine. He's fine, Lara's fine. I'd decided I would let him bring up the journal.

"Been writing," he said.

"Here and there. Some days it comes, some days it doesn't."

"I meant me," he said. Then slowly he paddled through a summary of how he'd been writing stories since I sent him one of mine (I'd forgotten this), and of reading dozens of story collections, and then of some dream he had, then, *finally*, of having his story accepted for publication (and two others, forthcoming). He sounded chagrined by the whole thing. "I told them to publish it as Seth Moxley but lines must've gotten crossed," he said. "Anyway, I'll put a copy in the mail today. If you get a chance to read it, I'd love to hear what you think."

"What happened to scuba diving?" I asked.

"I still dive. Lara and I are going down to the Pennecamp next week."

"Right, but—writing's not some hobby you just dabble in, Dad. It's not like scuba diving."

"I didn't say it was. You're the one who brought up diving." He inhaled deeply. "Why do you always do this?"

"Do what?"

"Make everything so damn difficult. I had to drink two glasses of wine before I called, just to relax. You were such an easygoing kid, you know that? Your mom used to call you Placido. I'd wake up panicked in the middle of the night and run to check on you, because you didn't make any noise."

"Maybe she was talking about the opera singer," I said.

Pause, a silent up-grinding of gears. "You don't remember much about your mother, do you?"

"A few things," I said.

"Her voice?"

"Not really."

"She had a terrific voice."

I didn't listen to much after that. Not because I'd already heard it, though I had—I wanted to collect a few things I remembered about her, instead of listening to his version again. Not facts or adjectives or secondhand details, but . . . qualities. Spliced-together images I could summon without words: her reaching without looking to take my hand in the street, the pockmarks on her wrist from the pins inserted when she broke her arm, her laughing, her crying, her warmth muted, her gone, dissolving room-by-room from our house. I'd never been able to write about her, not expressly. Whenever I tried, she emerged all white-robed and beatific, floating around, dispensing wisdom, laying doomed hands on me and everyone. Writing about her was imperfect remembering; it felt like a second death. I was far happier writing about fathers making sons help drag a deer to the roadside, saying, "Look into them fogged-up eyes. Now that's death, boy."

"She always had big plans for you," my father was saying. It was something he often said. I never asked him to be more specific.

It occurs to me that I'm breaking two of Hodgett's laws here. Never write about writing, and Never dramatize phone conversations. Put characters in the same room, he always said. See what they do when they can't hang up. "We'd love to see Carrie again," my father said after a while. "Any chance you'll be home for Christmas?"

Christmas was two months away. "We'll try," I told him.

After hanging up, I returned to my students' paragraphs, happy to marinate for a while in their simple insight. *My room is the special place*, Monica Mendez wrote. *Everywhere around me are shelfs of my memory things.*

•

Imagine a time for your characters, Hodgett used to say, when things might have turned out differently. Find the moment a choice was made that made other choices impossible. Readers like to see characters making choices.

She died in May. A week after the funeral, my father drives me and three friends to a theme park called Boardwalk and Baseball. He probably hopes it'll distract us for a few hours. All day long my friends and I ride roller coasters, take swings in the batting cage, eat hot dogs. I toss a Ping-Pong ball into a milk bottle and win a T-shirt. I can't even remember what kind of T-shirt it was, but I remember my glee after winning it.

My father follows us around and sits on a bench while we wait in line. He must be feeling pretty ruined but his son is doing just fine. His son is running from ride to ride, laughing it up with his friends. In fact, he hasn't thought about his mom once since they passed through the turnstiles.

My father is wearing sunglasses, to help with his allergies, he says. His sleeves are damp. I think he's been crying. "Having fun?" he keeps asking me.

I am, clearly I am. Sure, my mom died a week ago, but I just won a new T-shirt and my father gave each of us twenty dollars and the line to the Viper is really short and the sun is shining and I think we saw the girl from *Who's the Boss?*, or someone who looks a lot like her, in line at the popcorn cart.

I cringe when I remember this day. I want to revise everything. I want to come down with food poisoning, or lose a couple of fingers on the Raptor, something to mar the flawless good time I was having. Now I have to mar it in memory, I have to remember it with a black line through it.

"I'm glad you had fun," my father says on the drive home.

Our house is waiting for us when we get back. The failing spider plants on the front porch, the powder-blue envelopes in the mailbox.

●

November was a smear. Morning after morning I tried writing but instead played Etch-a-Sketch for two hours. I wrote a sentence. I waited. I stood up and walked around, thinking about the sentence. I leaned over the kitchen sink and ate an entire sleeve of graham crackers. I sat at my desk and stared at the sentence. I deleted it and wrote a different sentence. I returned to the kitchen and ate a handful of baby carrots. I began wondering about the carrots, so I dialed the toll-free number on the bag and spoke to a woman in Bakersfield, California.

"I would like to know where baby carrots come from," I said.

"Would you like the long version or the short version?" the woman asked.

For the first time in days, I felt adequately tended to. "Both," I said.

The short version: baby carrots are adult carrots cut into smaller pieces.

I returned to my desk, deleted my last sentence, and typed, "Babies are adults cut into smaller pieces." I liked this. I knew it would make an outstanding story, one that would win trophies and change the way people thought about fathers and sons if only I could find another three hundred or so sentences to follow it. But where were they?

•

A few weeks after my father sent me his first story, I received the winter issue of the *Longboat Quarterly* with a note: *Your father really wants to hear back from you about his story. He thinks you hated it. You didn't hate it, did you? XO, Lara.* No, Lara, I didn't. And I probably wouldn't hate this one, though I couldn't read past the title, "Blue Angels," without succumbing to the urge to sidearm the journal under my sofa (it took me four tries). I already knew what it was about.

Later, I sat next to Carrie on the sofa while she read it. Have you ever watched someone read a story? Their expression is dim and tentative at the beginning, alternately surprised and bewildered during the middle, and serene at the end. At least Carrie's was then.

"Well," she said when she was done. "How should we proceed?"

"Don't tell me. Just punch me in the abdomen. Hard." I pulled up my shirt, closed my eyes, and waited. I heard Carrie close the journal, then felt it lightly smack against my stomach. I read the story in the tub. Suffice it to say, it wasn't what I expected.

As a kid, I was obsessed with fighter planes. Tomcats, Super Hornets, anything with wings and missiles. I thought the story was going to be about my father taking me to see the Blue Angels, the U.S. Navy's flight team. It wouldn't have been much of a story: miserable heat, planes doing stunts, me in the autograph line for an hour, getting sunburned, and falling asleep staring at five jets on a poster as we drove home.

The story is about a widowed father drinking too much and deciding he needs to clean the house. He goes from room to room dusting, scrubbing floors, throwing things away. The blue angels are a trio of antique porcelain dolls my mother held on to from childhood. The man throws them away, then regrets it as soon as he hears the garbage truck driving off. The story ends with father and son at the dump, staring across vast hillocks of trash, paralyzed.

I remembered the dump, hot syrup stench, blizzard of birds overhead. He told me it was important to see where our trash ended up.

When I finished, I was sad again, nostalgic, and wanting to call my father. Which I did after drying off. Carrie sat next to me on the sofa with her legs over mine. "What are you doing?" she asked. I dialed the number, waited, listened to his answering-machine greeting—*Fred and Lara can't believe we missed your call*—and then hung up.

"Have I ever told you about when I saw the Blue Angels?" I asked Carrie.

"I don't think so."

"Well, get ready," I said.

●

I quit writing for a few weeks and went out into the world. I visited the airport, the beach, a fish camp, a cemetery, a sinkhole. I collected evidence, listened, tried to see past my impatience to the blood-radiant heart of things. I saw a man towing a woman on the handlebars of a beach cruiser. They were wearing sunglasses. They were poor. They were in love. I heard one woman say to another: *Everyone has a distinct scent, except me. Smell me, I don't have any scent.*

At the cemetery where my mother was buried, I came upon an old man lying very still on the ground in front of a headstone. When I walked by, I read the twin inscription. RUTH GOODINE 1920–1999, CHARLES GOODINE 1923–. "Don't mind me," the man said as I passed.

At my desk, I struggled to make something of this. I imagined what happened before and after. What moment made other moments impossible. He had come to the cemetery to practice for eternity. I could still picture him lying there in his gray suit, but the before and after were murky. Before, he'd been on a bus, or in a car, or a taxi. Afterward he would definitely go to . . . the supermarket to buy . . . lunch meat?

●

"Anything worth saying," Hodgett used to declare, "is unsayable. That's why we tell stories."

I returned to the cemetery. I walked from one end to the other, from the granite cenotaphs to the unmarked wooden headstones. Then I walked into the mausoleum and found my mother's placard, second from the bottom. I had to kneel down to see it. Another of Hodgett's six laws: Never dramatize a funeral or a trip to the cemetery. Too melodramatic, too obvious. I sat against something called the Serenity Wall and watched visitors mill in and out. They looked more inconvenienced than sad. My father and I used to come here, but at some point we quit. Afterward we'd go to a diner and he would say, "Order anything you want, anything," and I would order what I always ordered.

A woman with a camera asked if I could take her picture in front of her grandmother's placard. I said, "One, two, three, smile," and snapped her picture.

When the woman left, I said some things to my mom, all melodramatic, all obvious. In the months before she died, she talked about death like it was a long trip she was taking. She would watch over me, she said, if they let her. "I'm going to miss you," she said, which hadn't seemed strange until now. Sometimes I hoped she was watching me, but usually it was too terrible to imagine. "Here I am," I told the placard. I don't know why. It felt good, so I said it again.

"Why don't you talk about your mom?" Carrie asked me after I told her about going to the cemetery.

"You mean in general, or right now?"

Carrie didn't say anything. She had remarkable tolerance for waiting.

"What do you want to know?" I asked.

"Anything you tell me."

I forced a laugh. "I thought you were about to say, 'Anything you tell me is strictly confidential.' Like in therapy. Isn't that what they tell you in therapy?"

For some reason, I recalled my mother at the beach standing in the knee-deep water with her back to me. Her pants are wet to the waist and any deeper and her shirt will be soaked, too. I wondered why I needed to hoard this memory. Why did this simple static image seem like such a rare coin?

"Still waiting," Carrie said.

●

My father published two more stories in November, both about a man whose wife is dying of cancer. He had a weakness for depicting dreams, long, overtly symbolic dreams, and I found that the stories themselves read like dreams, I suffered them like dreams, and after a while I forgot I was reading. Like my high-school band teacher used to tell us, "Your goal is to stop seeing the notes." This never happened to me, every note was a seed I had to swallow, but now I saw what he meant.

Toward the end of the month, I was sick for a week. I canceled class and lay in bed, frantic with half-dreams. Carrie appeared, disappeared, reappeared. I picked up my father's stories at random and reread paragraphs out of order. I looked for repeated words, recurring details. One particular sentence called to me, from "Under the Light."

That fall the trees stingily held on to their leaves.

In my delirium, this sentence seemed to solve everything. I memorized it. I chanted it. I was the tree holding on to its leaves, but I couldn't let them go, because if I did I wouldn't have any more leaves. My father was waiting with a rake because that was his job, but I was being too stingy and weren't trees a lot like people?

I got better.

The morning I returned to class, Jacob Harvin from Prep Writing set a bag of Cheetos on my desk. "The machine gave me two by accident," he said.

I thanked him and began talking about subject-verb agreement. Out of the corner of my eye, I kept peeking at the orange Cheetos bag and feeling dreadful gratitude. "Someone tell me the subject in this sentence," I said, writing on the board. *"The trees of Florida hold on to their leaves."*

Terrie Inal raised her hand. "You crying, Mr. Moxley?" she asked.

"No, Terrie," I said. "I'm allergic to things."

"Looks like you're crying," she said. "You need a moment?"

The word *moment* did it. I let go. I wept in front of the class while they looked on horrified, bored, amused, sympathetic. "It's just, that was so *nice*," I explained.

Late in the week, my father called and I told him I was almost done with one of his stories. "Good so far," I said. Carrie suggested I quit writing for a while, unaware that I already had. I got drunk and broke my glasses. Someone wrote *Roach* with indelible marker on the hood of my car.

•

One day, I visited Harry Hodgett in his office. I walked to campus with a bagged bottle of Chivas Regal, his favorite, practicing what I'd say. Hodgett was an intimidating figure. He enjoyed playing games with you.

His door was open, but the only sign of him was an empty mug next to a student story. I leaned over to see *SBNI* written in the margin in Hodgett's telltale blue pen—it stood for *Sad But Not Interesting*—then I sat down. The office had the warm, stale smell of old books. Framed pictures of Hodgett and various well-known degenerates hung on the wall.

"This ain't the petting zoo," Hodgett said on his way in. He was wearing sweatpants and an Everlast T-shirt with frayed cut-off sleeves. "Who are you?"

Hodgett was playing one of his games. He knew exactly who I was. "It's me," I said, playing along. "Moxley."

He sat down with a grunt. He looked beat-up, baffled, winded, which meant he was in the early days of one of his sober sprees. "Oh yeah, Moxley, sure. Didn't recognize you without the . . . you know."

"Hat," I tried.

He coughed for a while, then lifted his trash can and expectorated into it. "So what are you pretending to be today?" he asked, which was Hodgett code for "So how are you doing?"

I hesitated, then answered, "Bamboo," a nice inscrutable thing to pretend to be. He closed his eyes, leaned his head back to reveal the livid scar under his chin, which was Hodgett code for "Please proceed." I told him all about my father. Knowing Hodgett's predilections, I exaggerated some things, made my father sound more abusive. Hodgett's eyes were shut, but I could tell he was listening by the way his face tic'ed and scowled. "He sends the stories out under my name," I said. "I haven't written a word in over a month."

To my surprise, Hodgett opened his eyes, looked at me as if he'd just awoken, and said, "My old man once tried to staple-gun a dead songbird to my scrotum." He folded his arms across his chest. "Just facts, not looking for pity."

I remembered reading this exact sentence—*staple-gun, songbird, scrotum*—then I realized where. "That happened to Moser," I said, "at the end of your novel *The Hard Road*. His dad wants to teach him a lesson about deprivation."

"That wasn't a novel, chief. That was first-person *life*." He huffed hoarsely. "All this business about literary journals and phone calls and hurt feelings, it's just not compelling. A story needs to sing like a wound. I mean, put your father and son in the same room together. Leave some weapons lying around."

"It isn't a story," I said. "I'm living it."

"I'm paid to teach students like you how to spoil paper. Look at me, man—I can barely put my head together." His face went through a series of contortions, like a ghoul in a mirror. "You want my advice," he said. "Go talk to the old man. Life ain't an opera. It's more like a series of commercials for things we have no intention of buying."

He narrowed his eyes, studying me. His eyes drooped; his mouth had white film at the corners. His nose was netted with burst capillaries.

"What happened to the young woman, anyway?" Hodgett asked. "The one with the nasty allure."

"You mean Carrie? My girlfriend?"

"Carrie, yeah. I used to have girlfriends like Carrie. They're fun."

He closed his eyes and with his right hand began casually kneading his crotch. "She did that story about the burn ward."

"Carrie doesn't write anymore," I said, trying to break the spell.

"Shame," Hodgett said. "Well, I guess that's how it goes. Talent realizes its limitations and gives up, while incompetence keeps plugging away until it has a book. I'd take incompetence over talent in a street fight any day of the week."

I picked up the Chivas Regal bottle and stood to leave. I studied the old man's big noisy battered redneck face. He was still fondling himself. I wanted to say something ruthless to him. I wanted my words to clatter around in his head all day, like his words did in mine. "Thanks," I said.

He nodded, pointed to the bottle. "You can leave that anywhere," he said.

●

Another memory: my mother, father, and me in our living room. I am eight years old. In the corner is the Christmas tree, on the wall are three stockings, on the kitchen table is a Styrofoam-ball snowman. We're about to open presents. My father likes to systematically inspect his to figure out what's inside. He picks up a flat parcel wrapped in silver paper, shakes it, turns it over, holds it to his ear, and says, "A book." He sets it on his lap and closes his eyes. "A . . . autobiography."

He's right every time.

My mother wears a yellow bathrobe and sits under a blanket.

She's cold again. She's sick but I don't know this yet. She opens her presents distractedly, saying *wow* and *how nice* and neatly folding the wrapping paper in half, then in quarters, while I tear into my gifts one after another. I say thanks without looking up.

That year, she and I picked out a new diver's watch for

my father, which we wait until all the presents have been opened to give him. We've wrapped it in a small box and then wrapped that box inside a much larger one.

I set it in front of him. He looks at me, then her. He lifts the box. "Awfully light." He shakes it, knocks on each of the box's six sides. "Things are not what they seem."

My mother begins coughing, softly at first—my father pauses, sets his hands flat atop the box—then uncontrollably, in big hacking gusts. I bring her water, which she drinks, still coughing. My father helps her to the bathroom and I can hear her in there, gagging and hacking. For some reason, I'm holding the remote control to the television.

The box sits unopened in the living room for the rest of the day. At night, with Mom in bed and me brushing my teeth, he picks it up, says, "Diver's watch, waterproof up to a hundred meters," then opens it.

•

Carrie and I drove to Vero Beach the day before Christmas Eve. There seemed to be a surplus of abandoned cars and dead animals on the side of the road and, between this and the gray sky and the homemade signs marking off the fallow farms—PREPARE FOR THE RAPTURE, PRAISE HIM—I began to daydream about the apocalypse. I was hoping it would arrive just like this, quietly, without much warning or fanfare.

"I know it's fiction," Carrie was saying, referring to my father's most recent story, "but it's hard not to read it as fact.

Did you actually tape pictures of your mom to the front door when Lara came over the first time?"

"Maybe," I said. "Probably. I don't really remember."

I taped the pictures in a circle, like the face of a clock. I waited at the top of the stairs for the doorbell to ring.

Carrie pointed to a billboard featuring the likeness of a recently killed NASCAR driver's car, flanked by white angel wings. "I hope they haven't started letting race cars into heaven," she said.

●

I finally talked to my father about his writing while we were in the garage looking for the Styrofoam-ball snowman. We were searching through boxes, coming across yearbooks, macramé owls, clothes, and my oboe, snug in purple velvet. I always forgot how fit and reasonable-looking my father was until I saw him in person. His hair was now fully gray and his silver-rimmed reading glasses sat low on his nose.

"I didn't know we went to the dump to hunt for those dolls," I said. It sounded more reproachful than I meant it to.

He looked up from the box, still squinting, as if he'd been searching dark, cramped quarters. "You mean the story?"

" 'Blue Angels,' " I said. "I read it. I read all of them, actually."

"That's surprising," he said, folding the flaps of the box in front of him. "Best not to make too much out of what happens in stories, right?"

"But you were looking for those dolls."

"I didn't expect to find them. I wanted to see where they ended up." He shook his head. "It's hard to explain. After your mom died—I'd be making breakfast and my mind would wander to Annie and I'd start to lose it. The only time I relaxed was when I slept. That's why I started studying dreams. I found that if I did a few exercises before falling asleep, I could dictate what I dreamed about. I could remember. I could pause and fast-forward and rewind. You're giving me a 'how pitiful' look."

"It's just strange," I said. "The dreams, the stories, it feels like I haven't been paying attention. I had no idea you were being all quietly desperate while I was waiting for my toast."

"It wasn't all the time." He pushed his glasses up on his nose and looked at me. "You should try writing about her, if you haven't already. You find yourself unearthing all sorts of things. Stories are just like dreams."

Something about his advice irritated me. It brought to mind his casually boastful author's note, *This is his first published story.* "Stories aren't dreams," I said.

"They're not? What are they, then?"

I didn't know. All I knew was that if he thought they were dreams, then they had to be something else. "They're jars," I said. "Full of bees. You unscrew the lid and out come the bees."

"All right," he said, moving the box out of his way. "But I

still think you should try writing about her. Even if it means the bees coming out."

We searched until I found the snowman resting face-down in a box of embroidered tablecloths. A rat or weasel had eaten half of his head, but he still smiled his black-beaded smile.

"I remember when you made that," my father said.

I did, too. That is, I remembered *when* I made it, without remembering the actual making of it. I made it with my mom when I was three. Every year it appeared in the center of the kitchen table and every year she would say, "You and I made that. It was raining outside and you kept saying, 'Let's go stand in the soup.'" Maybe she thought that if she reminded me enough, I'd never forget the day we made it, and maybe I didn't, for a while.

I brought the snowman into the house and showed it to Carrie, who was sitting in the living room with Lara. "Monstrous," Carrie said.

Lara was looking at me significantly. An unfinished popcorn string dangled from her lap. "Carrie was sharing her thoughts on your dad's stories," she said. "Do you want to add anything?" My father walked into the living room holding two mismatched candlesticks.

"They," I said slowly, looking at Carrie, waiting for her to mouth the words . . . "were" . . . she really was lovely, not just lovely-looking, but lovely . . . "good." I breathed and said, "They were good."

Carrie applauded. "He means it, too," she said. "That slightly nauseous look on his face, that's sincerity." Then to me: "Now that wasn't so hard. Don't you feel light now, the weight lifted?"

I felt as if I'd swallowed a stone. I felt it settling and the moss starting to cover it.

"Frederick here's the real writer," my father said. "I'm just dabbling."

How humble, right? How wise and fatherly and kind. But I know what he meant: Frederick here's the fraud. He's the hack ventriloquist. I'm just dabbing at his wounds.

●

What more should be said about our visit? I want to come to my father's Mexico story without too much flourish. I hear Hodgett's voice: Never end your story with a character realizing something. Characters shouldn't realize things: readers should. But what if the character is also a reader?

We decorated the tree. We strung lights around the sago palms in the front yard. We ate breakfast in an old sugar mill and, from the pier, saw a pod of dolphins rising and rolling at dawn. I watched my father, tried to resist the urge to catalog him. His default expression was benign curiosity. He and Lara still held hands. They finished each other's sentences. They seemed happy. Watching my father watch the dolphins, I felt like we were at an auction, bidding on the same item. It was an ugly, miserly feeling.

I couldn't sleep on Christmas Eve. Carrie and I shared my old bedroom, which now held a pair of single beds separated by my old tricolor nightstand. All the old anxieties were coming back, the deadness of a dark room, the stone-on-stone sound of a crypt top sliding closed as soon as I began drifting to sleep.

I heard Carrie stir during the night. "I can't sleep," I said.

"Keep practicing," she said groggily. "Practice makes practice."

"I was wondering why you quit writing. You had more talent than all of us. You always made it look so easy."

She exhaled through her nose and moved to face me. I could just barely see her eyes in the dark. "Let's pretend," she said.

I waited for her to finish. When she didn't, I said, "Let's pretend what?"

"Let's pretend two people are lying next to each other in a room. Let's pretend they're talking about one thing and then another. It got too hard to put words in their mouths. They stopped cooperating."

She rolled over, knocked her knee against the wall. "They started saying things like, I'm hungry, I'm thirsty, I need air. I'm tired of being depicted. I want to live."

I thought about her burn-ward story, the way boys were on one side of the room and girls were on the other. Before lights-out, the nurse came in and made everyone sing and then closed a curtain to separate the boys from the girls.

After a while, I said, "You sleeping?" She didn't answer, so I went downstairs.

I poured a glass of water, and looked around my father's office for something to read. On his desk were a dictionary, a thesaurus, and something called *The Yellow Emperor's Classic of Internal Medicine,* which I flipped through. *When a man grows old his bones become dry and brittle like straw and his eyes bulge and sag.* I opened the top drawer of his filing cabinet and searched through a stack of photocopied stories until I found a stapled manuscript titled "Mexico Story." I sat down on his loveseat and read it.

In Mexico, it began, *some men still remember Pancho Villa.* I prepared for a thinly veiled account of my father and Lara's vacation, but the story, it turned out, followed a man, his wife, and their son on vacation in Mexico City. They've traveled there because the mother is sick and their last hope is a healer rumored to help even the most hopeless cases. The family waits in the healer's sitting room for their appointment. The son, hiding under the headphones of his new Walkman, just wants to go home. The mother tries to talk to him but he just keeps saying, *Huh? Huh?*

The three of us go into a dim room, where the healer asks my mother what's wrong, what her doctors said, why has she come. Then he shakes his head and apologizes. "Very bad," he says. He tells a rambling story about Pancho Villa, which none of us listens to, then reaches into a drawer and pulls out a wooden back-scratcher. He runs it up and down along my mother's spine.

"How's that feel?" he asks.

"Okay," the mother says. "Is it doing anything?"

"Not a thing. But it feels good, yes? It's yours to keep, no charge."

I must have fallen asleep while reading, because at some point the threads came loose in the story and mother, father, and son leave Mexico for a beach that looks a lot like the one near our house. Hotels looming over the sea oats. The inlet lighthouse just visible in the distance. I sit on a blanket next to my father while my mother stands in knee-deep water with her back to us.

"She's sick," my father says. "She doesn't want me to say anything, but you're old enough to know. She's really . . . sick."

If she's sick she shouldn't be in the water, I think. Her pedal pushers are wet to the waist, and if she wades in any deeper, her shirt will be soaked, too. I pick up a handful of sand and let it fall through my fingers.

"So it's like a battle," he's saying. "Good versus bad. As long as we stick together, we'll get through it okay."

My mother walks out of the water. She is bathed in light and already I can barely see her. She sits next to us, puts her hand on my head, and, in the dream, I realize this is one of those moments I need to prolong. I put my hand over hers and hold it there. I push down on her hand until it hurts and I keep pushing.

"You can let go," she says. "I'm not going anywhere."

The next morning I found my father in checked pajamas near the Christmas tree. He carefully stepped over a stack of presents onto the tree skirt and picked up a gift from Carrie and me. He shook it and listened. He tapped on it with his finger.

"It's not a watch," I said.

He turned to me and smiled. "I've narrowed it down to two possibilities," he said.

"Here." He waved me over. "Sit down, I've got something for you."

I sat on the couch and he handed me a long, flat package wrapped in red-and-white paper. "Wait, wait," he said when I started to unwrap it. "Guess what it is first."

I looked at it. All that came to mind was a pair of chop-sticks.

"Listen," he said, taking it from me. He held it up to my ear and shook it. "Don't think, just listen. What's that sound like to you?"

I didn't hear anything. "I don't hear anything," I said.

He continued shaking the gift. "It's trying to tell you what it is. Hear it?"

I waited for it, I listened. "No."

He tapped the package against my head. "Listen harder," he said.

buzzers

Soon after Andrew left the hospital for the airport, he knew his father would die, and that's exactly
what he did. His mother was sleeping on a foldout
chair while Dora, his little sister, sat on a stool studying her father's respirator. She was cycling through
the machines again, figuring out which worked and
which did not. The heart monitor appeared to be
working, but the respirator left her skeptical, some-

thing in the way the rubber flue trembled as it collapsed and bloomed, collapsed and bloomed. Her father was expending every last bit of energy, vigor, whatever it was, to keep the machines alive.

When the heart monitor flatlined and her father let out a last long sigh, she stood up and walked over to the side of his bed. Another machine began emitting a series of agitated beeps, and she touched his shoulder, still warm beneath his sweatshirt, and his hair, which felt like hair, of course, but she wanted to be sure. She wasn't afraid. She was ready. She'd seen a movie where a woman places coins atop her dead husband's closed eyelids. Dora liked this, but her father was on his side. He looked happy, she decided. Plus she didn't have any coins.

She noticed that on her father's forehead, shining under the muted glow of the overhead track lights, was a single red speck of party glitter, which, when she shifted her view, pulsed like a tiny cinder. Quickly, before the doctor arrived, she used her fingernail to remove it. Holding it on her finger, she hesitated to let it fall to the floor. She wasn't superstitious, but flicking the glitter to the floor seemed like an improper thing to do. How had it ended up here, and what had it celebrated? She could feel her confidence disappearing. She had no idea what to do with the glitter. A doctor and two nurses in breast cancer T-shirts came into the room and checked her father's pulse. Her mother sat up. "What is it now?" she said.

Her mother and the doctor went into the bathroom,

where Dora heard the awful pull of the chain-light. The nurses began printing and tearing readouts from some of the machines, and Dora thought: receipts.

She searched his face. It looked gray, with an expression that was not calm or serene or undisturbed—but gone. She wouldn't cry; she had already cried. Crying now would be a big step backward. She could wail, or keen. People still keened, didn't they? She reached under the covers and held her father's hand, cold. Room temperature, but cold. The moment she touched it she wanted to let go, but the nurses were watching, so she held on. She imagined something un-spooling like anchor-chain inside of her and trailing after him wherever he was going. Away, away. Now would be an ideal time to keen, but it wasn't the kind of thing you willed your way into, you just did it, which was why Dora wouldn't be able to do it.

She asked one of the nurses for his ID bracelet. The nurse looked to the other nurse, who wasn't paying attention, and then quickly and efficiently clipped off the bracelet and handed it to Dora.

She looked at her finger and saw the glitter had vanished, and she was relieved. She had lately become a careful reader of signs and this seemed a very good sign.

●

In the airport, Andrew tried not to move while the hand-wand made excited noises above his belt buckle, once, twice, three times. When the security guard was finished, he asked if the belt cost a lot of money. Andrew told him that it was his father's, so he didn't know, and the guard said, "In my experience, things that look expensive usually are."

He walked with a group from his design class to the gate. They wore dark simple clothes and tried to project a European uniformity. Andrew bought a newspaper and sat at the gate reading an article about a red tide on the Gulf Coast. Red tide, the article said, was caused by algae blooms, which attacked marine life and turned the water a rusty color. The article called the algae "toxic salt-loving algae," and made it seem dastardly and inexorable, like death itself.

Seated around him were his classmates, the future architects of the world, on their way to Vicenza, Italy, for a month-long course in city planning. Andrew had always wanted to be an architect, even before he knew what architects did—especially before he knew what they did. *Architect.* It sounded smart, upstanding, conclusive. People warned that the program was hard work, but it wasn't. It was long work. Stare, sketch, hold wooden dowels together while the glue dries, stare some more, sketch some more, solder. His finished models looked more like a building's circuit board than an actual building. Defending them during pinup, Andrew would point out subdominant structures and transparent intersections. "What I'm investigating is the junction of these lozenges here at the center," he would say. And: "What I'm investigating is the conversation between opposing inser-

tions." And: "What I'm investigating is the way space ne-
gates space." And: "What I'm investigating are tones."

Of course, of course, his classmates said. Many of their
models were doing the very same thing.

The trip to Vicenza was standard for students entering
their third year. In Vicenza, the Renaissance architect Palla-
dio had designed basilicas and villas for the aristocracy, turning the city into his personal design lab. There, the professors
wanted the students to be aware of *relationships*, both particular to Vicenza and universal to human occupation. That's
what they said. Andrew waited for them to elaborate, but
they said no more. Sometimes he found their cryptic instruc-
tions interesting, even exciting, and other times—currently,
for instance—they seemed negligent, a way of alluding to a
world without the burden of making sense of it.

Nonetheless, he was eager to go. He'd never been on a
long flight or to Europe, so the minute he stepped onto the
plane he would find himself on unfamiliar territory. This
was one of the reasons people traveled, he guessed, to go
from the known to the unknown, a thing he'd never longed
for until now. "Over my dead body," his father said when
Andrew asked if he should forgo the trip. It was meant to be
a joke, but no one, including Andrew's father, had laughed.
What Andrew wanted right now was to be where he couldn't
understand a word.

Aboard the airplane before takeoff, he sat in a middle
seat away from the rest of the group, between an older couple

who seemed to be traveling together. They traded excited comments about the complimentary purple socks they were given. Both of them freed the socks from the plastic and put them on. Andrew kept his in his lap atop the Walter Benjamin book he'd been carrying around for the past month. The woman, who sat to his left, asked his name and he told her. He asked if she wanted to switch seats with him and she said she did not. "We'll have plenty of time to sit next to each other in Athens," she said. "Athens, Greece."

This conversation starter, if that's what it was, went unheeded by Andrew. He wanted to put on his headphones and read Walter Benjamin until he fell asleep, but didn't want to appear rude. He waited for the woman to elaborate. She wore long clip-on earrings that jiggled as she rooted around in her pocketbook. To his right, the man wrapped his old socks in the plastic and was trying to figure out what to do with them.

After a few minutes, the woman leaned forward and said, "I never finished telling you about Annie. Where was I?"

"Tongue cancer," the man said.

"Can you imagine anything more gruesome? I didn't even know one could get cancer of the tongue."

"It's an organ like everything else. It's got cells."

"It must be new," the woman said.

Andrew opened the book. He read, "There was the pedestrian who wedged himself into the crowd, but there was also the *flâneur* who demanded elbow room and was unwilling to forgo the life of the gentleman of leisure." He closed the book. He watched the flight attendants walk back and forth preparing the plane. They were solemn and purposeful, but when a passenger requested something, the attendants brightened while tilting their heads to show utmost receptiveness.

One of them came by and said, "Please remember to turn off all electronic devices before we push back from the gate."

The woman asked the attendant how many pilots there were on a transatlantic flight like this one, while Andrew reached into his pocket to turn off his phone. It had already been turned off. When he turned it on again, he saw that a message was waiting. It was from his mother. An echoing sigh. "It's happened," she said.

The woman next to Andrew was now holding the attendant's arm to fix her in place. She asked if all four of the pilots were copilots, like cocaptains on a bridge team, or if one was a main pilot and the other three were copilots, or if they were all simply pilots, and would it be too much trouble to get a small glass of tonic water for her and her husband before the plane took off? Tonic water settled the stomach.

"I hope you get this," Andrew's mother said.

When the message ended, a digitized voice gave him numeric options. On the cover of Walter Benjamin was a picture of a glass-roofed arcade below a much smaller picture of a woman's face. It was a pensive face, not necessarily kind-looking, but full of thought, especially in the vicinity of the mouth. Only half of the face was visible in the frame, and if

Andrew's first impulse wasn't to hurry and gather his things and exit the plane and make his way back to Orlando to be with his mother and Dora, maybe it was because he wanted a few more minutes to figure out this woman's face.

At the start of his second year, his instructors recommended that he find a single philosopher whose ideas he approved of. Not to let the philosopher's ideas impose themselves too rigidly on what he was building, but to think of them, the ideas, as a miner's helmet, the light by which he sees what he's building . . .

Andrew was still holding the phone to his ear, he realized. "For more options, press star," the digitized voice repeated, another group of words that hadn't yet cohered into anything that made sense.

It's happened. He knew that if he stayed in his seat a little while longer, it would be too late to do anything. In a few minutes the bay doors would close, the plane would leave the gate, take off, and, seven hours later, land in London. He would call his mother from a pay phone in the airport while waiting for the connecting flight and explain that he didn't get her message until it was too late. He thought: in a few minutes the doors will close and I won't have to make a decision. I'll be locked in transit, trapped.

He opened the in-flight magazine and mentally filled in the crossword puzzle. Both the husband and wife, he could tell, were watching him, so he turned the page. As he read an article about the steakhouses of Denver, he decided that if he came across the word *yes*, he would tell the flight attendant he needed to get off the plane. But if he found the word *no*, he would stay on the plane. Searching the page, he found *no* once, twice, again, again.

As if to further confirm things, the man on his right offered him a piece of gum. It was the kind that came on a bubbled sheet of plastic, like sore-throat drops, and when Andrew accepted the offer, the man expertly pressed two through the foil into his hand. He leaned over and pressed out two more pieces for his wife, who declared, "We'll all have the same breath!"

•

Andrew's father first went to the hospital on Halloween morning. He'd eaten scallops for dinner and was up all night with what he thought was food poisoning. The doctors decided to keep him overnight for tests. When Andrew and his mother and sister visited him, the hospital staff was wearing costumes over their uniforms: pirate orderlies and vampire nurses. Andrew thought hospitals were impervious to things like Halloween, but in walked his father's doctor, dressed in a cowboy hat and boots. "Howdy everyone," he said. This put none of them at ease.

His father was scanned and biopsied. He was given a prognosis and sent home with a hospital pocket calendar filled in with four months of appointments. The prognosis, as told to Dora and Andrew: Dad'll be visiting the hospital for at least four more months. After that, things proceeded very slowly. From one day to the next he looked and acted more or less the same, but if Andrew compared him with a picture from before he got sick, the difference was startling. He looked thinner, of course, and shorter. Everything about him seemed reduced in scale, even his bathrobe, his meals. For breakfast he ate a handful of raisins; dinner was a slice of toast.

For half his life he managed the jai alai fronton. His co-workers there brought tamales to the house, one pan after another. It became a joke between his mother and father. "I say we start freezing them," his father would say. "Store them and thaw them out years from now to see what they tell us." There were cheese tamales and turkey tamales and breakfast tamales. His mother cleaned the tamale pans and returned them filled with cookies.

Whenever Andrew went to a restaurant, he found himself looking for scallops on the menu. He hated scallops. He hated the word, *scallops*. It sounded like a disease in itself.

Every so often he allowed himself to imagine his father being around in ten, fifteen years, but even before he was admitted to Fourth West, everyone had resigned themselves to the worst. Andrew saw how his father seemed to be attending to last things, boxing up old clothes, calling friends he'd lost contact with. There was a slight, barely noticeable shift of balance in the house. His mother became quieter, his father louder, more erratic.

Andrew left for college, a four-hour drive. He was distracted from his schoolwork for a while, and then he was so busy he had no choice but to be swallowed up by it. He enjoyed the dull repetitiveness of studio work, making things out of other things. He went to a party where one of his female classmates said to him, "My father's dying, too." He didn't know if she was offering sympathy or trying to start a conversation. How casually she said it, as if pointing out they were wearing the same brand of sneakers.

When his father was moved to Fourth West, Andrew drove home to help decorate the room and prop get-well cards on the end tables. "He isn't going to get better here," Dora predicted. He returned to school and waited, and Dora and his mother waited at home. They celebrated Thanksgiving at Fourth West, behind the sliding blue-and-white curtain, Christmas. Another shift: his father began complaining about the waiting, implying that anything would be preferable, anything. There's been a mistake, he would say. He had waited too long, the whole family had. They waited and waited until waiting was a place they had gone for good.

•

About a half hour later, after the pilot had twice announced, "Should be a few more minutes," the plane was still parked at the gate. Andrew read every word of the in-flight magazine, including the letters to the editor. He was interested in the kind of person who'd write a letter to an in-flight magazine. It seemed a sincere and hopeful act. One of the letters began, "For years my wife and I have been enjoying the unlikely grandeur of Quito." Below the letter-writer's name was his e-mail address, which Andrew jotted down on the flyleaf of Walter Benjamin. He thought that maybe he would write the man a letter about his letter.

He imagined his mother sitting by a phone, hand poised over the receiver, waiting. The correct, the only thing for him to do was to start making his way home. If he could just stand up, grab his bag, and get off the plane, he knew he could manage the rest of it. The preparations, the funeral, picking over the remains of the unmade summer with his mother and Dora. He just had to spark the right neurons to tell the right muscles what needed to be done. But the thought of asking the woman to unbuckle her seat belt and stand up so that he could stand up, and then standing up and fishing his bag out of the overhead compartment and walking down the aisle had begun to make him very, very tired.

As a kid, he read a book about an astronaut who orbits the earth for a few weeks and returns to find that eighty years have passed and everyone he loves is dead. It was a sad story made sadder by the astronaut going back into space and deciding not to come back. There was something sweet and fitting about the hopelessness of the astronaut, alone in his space capsule. Riding the bus home from school, Andrew would try to summon this feeling by pretending his family was gone and that he'd decided to live out his days on a bus. Sometimes, to complete the illusion, he waited until the final stop to get off the bus and would have to spend a half hour walking home. He remembered doing it several times, so it must have been worth it.

Tory from his Building Arts class stopped by Andrew's seat on his way to the bathroom. He was wearing a black T-shirt on which MOORE IS LESS was printed in white letters, a design joke. "We wondered where you were," he said. "Why are you stranded way back here in steerage?"

Andrew told him he didn't know, that this was the seat that was printed on his boarding pass. "I'm happy back here," he said.

"The woman next to me took some pills and went stiff about thirteen seconds later. Her mouth's wide-ass open. She looks dead."

"What are you talking about?"

Tory looked at the man next to Andrew, then at the woman. "If she ever wakes up, you two could switch. It's gonna be a long flight."

When Tory left, the woman asked who he was and Andrew told her. She said, "I bet he's not very popular, although everyone knows who he is."

Andrew didn't agree or disagree, though she was right.

"I can tell," she said. "The instant he opened his mouth, I said to myself, here is someone who's talked his way into being ignored."

This, too, seemed an accurate observation. "You're probably right."

"Watch out," the man said. "My wife's a great authority on other people."

"Instincts," the woman said.

"When it comes to other people my wife could win contests."

"Years ago when we were visiting Japan, a very old woman on the subway came up to me and handed me a sheet of paper with some Japanese written on it. The concierge at our hotel translated it. 'You are a lamp in a world of lampshades.' Isn't that wonderful?"

"It was an advertisement for a new kind of shampoo," the man whispered to Andrew. He could smell the dank spearmint of the gum they were all chewing. The man opened and closed the window shade on the view of the terminal. "Any thoughts on our friend here?" he asked his wife.

"We haven't even left the gate."

"But you've formed an opinion. Nine seconds she says it takes," he told Andrew.

Andrew looked at the woman, who nodded with her eyes closed as if she'd foreseen the question. A sharp line ran down her chin from each side of her mouth, like a ventriloquist's doll. She said, "Serious. Kindhearted. Has a bit of the lone wolf to him. A bit of the constant traveler. He's resilient, no, *resistant*. If he finds something he likes at a restaurant, he'll happily order it every time. He's practical. But he needs things a certain way."

"His way," the husband said. "That can be admirable."

Stand up, and you'll never see these two again, Andrew was thinking. Stand up, and you'll be doing the correct, the only thing.

"We're making him uncomfortable, Reed." The woman patted the armrest as if it were his leg. "The poor boy probably can't wait to go sit with his friends."

"It's okay," Andrew said.

"Even when she's not listening, she's listening," the man said. "It's like living with a detective."

The two said nothing else until the plane began backing out of the gate. Neither did Andrew, whose body was fixed rigid to the seat, a prop for the Walter Benjamin and the complimentary purple socks in his lap. He wasn't going anywhere. By staying still he could feel himself being pulled away, like how an ocean undercurrent tows you up the beach, easily, unnoticed, past hotel front after hotel front, until you've forgotten which one you were using to keep your place . . .

He thought about how his father called the screeching crows perched on his window ledge *buzzers*, which was what Dora called buzzards.

How he'd begun wearing calfskin driving gloves in the hospital, and would mark pauses in conversation by fastening and unfastening the Velcro.

How, especially how, Andrew had walked into the wrong house the last time he returned home from school. His mother and sister still lived in the townhouse where he grew up, in a subdivision of two-story luxury townhouses around a man-made lake. The townhouses were built five to a building, with the three middle units exactly the same and the two end units mirror images of each other.

It was late and he hadn't slept much. He climbed stairs he'd climbed a thousand times, but instead of turning right he turned left. The door was unlocked and Andrew walked into the foyer and waited for his eyes to adjust to the darkened house. He noticed an unfamiliar pale-oak bookshelf in the living room, which, since he hadn't been home in a while, didn't seem all that unusual. Only when he approached it to look at a framed photograph, which turned out to be of his neighbor, old Mr. Patterson, shaking hands with a man dressed up as Captain America, did he realize what had happened. But not before he thought, *What is this picture doing in our house?*

Then, as now, he couldn't bring himself to move. He looked around and tried to figure out what was different between this townhouse and his. A white cat was sleeping on the back of a white couch, a coffee table, a mug with a straw in it. At eye level on the sliding glass door were pictures of pelicans, which Andrew remembered seeing from the other side, years ago. His father had explained that the pelicans were there so Mr. Patterson didn't accidentally slam into the sliding glass door while drunk. The carpet was white, like the cat; one of the walls was filled with black-and-white photographs. He felt pinned into place.

"Defamiliarize yourselves," his instructors had said. "Don't overlook what you've seen before, or *think* you've seen before, because you've seen it before. See things again for the first time."

There was Mr. Patterson yelling. There was Mr. Patterson holding a nightstick in the doorway. "Identify yourself!" he was yelling.

When Andrew did, and Mr. Patterson finally calmed himself down, he returned the nightstick to his umbrella stand and sat down on the couch. The cat hopped to the coffee table to a chair to the dining-room table, never touching the carpet. "What the hell were you doing just standing there? What were your plans?"

Andrew tried to explain. It was late, he hadn't slept much. Mr. Patterson, in a tank top and a pair of boxer shorts too small for him, smiled right through the explanation. Below the hem of his shorts peeked the stingy-looking cap of his penis. "You need to realize," he said, still smiling, "that I would've had every right, every right in the world, to brain you."

He sounded sort of disappointed that he hadn't.

Andrew apologized and Mr. Patterson said something complimentary about his father, talking about him in the past tense, and Andrew thanked him.

"I know your daddy's sick, but you can't go standing in other people's houses. You've got to keep your wits about you. When my wife died I moved here to Florida. Most people come to Florida to die, but I came here to live. That's what I say when somebody asks why I'm taking skydiving lessons. Death happens to the dead. We're here to live!"

Andrew knew that this was self-mythologizing nonsense (and who needed *lessons* to jump out of an airplane?) but he didn't say anything. He just wanted to explain what had happened so that Mr. Patterson would understand. It sounded sensible until the part where he realized he was in the wrong house. Mr. Patterson had watched him, Andrew, staring through his own face like a zombie, he said. I haven't been sleeping much, Andrew kept saying. We have the same floor plan. Haven't you ever woken up before your body?

Mr. Patterson smiled, his penis perched close to his leg like a pilot fish. Probably he was still marveling at how righteous it would've been to brain Andrew with that nightstick. Andrew might as well have been explaining how he was just trying to defamiliarize himself and see things again for the first time. It's an assignment, he could've told Mr. Patterson. For school.

This was the visit when his father wore the calfskin gloves. His face looked rummaged but the gloves were brand-new, toast-colored. Andrew sat on the pullout sofa and waited while his father pulled on the Velcro and stared out at the window ledge, which was fixed with metal spikes to deter birds. Snip, snip, snip. A trio of crows had worked their way around the spikes and huddled with their tail feathers against the window, screeching into the wind. "You might fool other birds," his father said finally. "But you never can fool the buzzers. Buzzers won't pretend to pretend."

Although he'd heard what his father said and knew what he meant, Andrew said, "What?" Maybe he wanted to see if he'd repeat it. He didn't. It was as if he'd been working over this idea for months and, once he said it, wasn't about to spoil it by saying it again.

He continued the routine with the gloves. Andrew continued waiting.

•

On the airplane, which was slowly backing out of the gate, his stomach tightened and he suddenly felt short of breath. His father was gone and he should've gotten off the plane. His father was gone and he'd failed to do the correct thing. He'd failed to do anything.

"At last," the man next to him said as the plane inched closer to the runway. He opened the window shade and his wife leaned over Andrew and made a relieved sound. Andrew tucked the Walter Benjamin into the seat pocket, closed his eyes, and tried to breathe. He thought about why he was going to Vicenza, what his instructors expected him to look for: relationships, specific to the city, universal to human occupation. The open-endedness of this was comforting, the improbability of searching very long without discovering it.

"Sit back and enjoy the rest of your flight," the flight attendant announced once the plane had reached cruising altitude. "May we suggest trying on your complimentary travel socks?"

Just as the husband and wife had done earlier, Andrew slipped off his shoes and socks and replaced them with the travel socks, which felt cheap and warm and new. He sat up and saw several other passengers doing the same thing. Travel socks, he'd never heard of such a thing, but he liked the sound of it.

There was a TV installed in the seat back facing him, and on it he watched famous people laughing. Something inconceivably funny was going on. He could still feel a tightening in his stomach and it occurred to him that, although he was traveling far from home, he'd soon be met with what had happened. No matter how far he went, it would find him there.

A little while later, the woman next to Andrew reached over and tapped her husband on the shoulder. He stirred awake and asked what she wanted. "Ever since I heard about Annie's cancer, my own tongue's felt too big for my mouth," she told him, "like it has no business being in there at all."

She stuck out her tongue and began moving it back and forth.

"You'll get used to it again," her husband said, and went back to sleep.

in the pines

For the third time Alta was free. Free of obligation and free of men and free of her home of ten years, a palm-log cabin with two dining rooms. She was seventy-four years old but she still felt like a young woman. Long ago she'd foreseen the day when time's advance would collapse her into a dry heap, but that day hadn't come, not yet.

Her new apartment was small and had wall-to-wall carpet with a chaotic pattern, but the view was nice. Her back patio looked out onto a Civil War battlefield returned to its native state: treeless and shaggy with grass that on windy afternoons was wonderful to watch. Sections of grass zigzagged open as gusts of wind swept through. If she positioned herself just right, all she saw was the vast expanse of grass, ceaseless as the sea. No houses, no landscaping, nothing but drab, irregular movement. It reminded her of home.

She'd lived on the Florida coast for fifty years, until recently, when she, too, had been returned to her native state. Pennsylvania, pill-shaped hilly patch of zilch. Her great-niece and great-nephew lived somewhere nearby. When her third husband, George, died, they came to Florida and helped Alta move to In the Pines, not a nursing home, they insisted, a *retirement village*. Not a shelter for the suddenly senile and abruptly decrepit but a community of *active seniors*.

Wow! they said, following Alta down the hall and pointing out the exercise room, the computer room, the activity room. Hey now! Maybe *we* should think about living here! In her apartment, they asked where she wanted the dining-room table. "The dining room," she told them, but there was no dining room. They helped unpack her clothes, programmed her VCR, cleaned the sliding glass door.

"What a view," said her great-niece, a blithely confident girl named Brenna. She held back the curtains. "You'd think you were in the middle of the woods, Aunt Alta. Except that phone tower."

Alta went to the patio door and looked out. Far beyond the battlefield, tethered vertical by just-visible cables, was the gunmetal tower, red beacon lights blinking. Alta cropped it out by centering her view on the middle of the battlefield. In Florida, she used to sit in a beach chair close to the ocean and let the tide run beneath her. She continued waiting, waiting . . . for what, she didn't remember, or never knew. Her husband, maybe, to come tell her it was time to go. To put his hand on her shoulder, tap his wedding band against her clavicle, and reset her to normal.

"It appears," Alta said in her new apartment, "that I need a man."

Her great-niece and great-nephew hesitated, and then, together, they laughed. Alta was their favorite aunt, the one who knew just how to defuse an awkward moment. While the mood was bright, they hung Alta's new apartment key on a metal hook marked KEYS, and then excused themselves.

•

She ate pancakes with five others at her table, two men and three women who stared at her like dogs at an empty food bowl while she spoke. For weeks she'd been trying to interest the two men, offering easy questions like *Anyone been outside today?* and *Anyone play cards?* One man belched wetly into his cloth napkin, while the other clutched a biscuit and crumpled his face into a deep sort of personal frown, as if straining his bowels. Alta, who'd been married, and widowed, three times, had always relied on men to measure her own well-being—and, in better days, to enlarge it—and this, this dim unanimous disregard, was not good.

"Wasn't our year," one of the men said to the other.

"It never is," the other said. "I hate to admit it, but we're a national joke."

"This year we are. What's next year look like?"

"What do you think?"

"Same as this year."

"Same as last year," the second man said, "same as *every* year."

Alta thought this the most dismal conversation she'd ever heard. "That's an awful way to talk," she said to them.

A few moments later, though, she realized they were just complaining about a sports team. She excused herself and left the table, but the low feeling stayed with her, shadowing her as she walked the asphalt nature trail around the man-made lake, in the center of which fountains made daisies of water. She passed dozens of memorial trees and their scuffed little markers. The younger trees were tethered upright like the phone tower behind her apartment, and Alta's thoughts drifted as she looked over the names, former residents of In the Pines. What if the dead residents were actually buried inside the trees? She imagined beavers padding through at night and, unaware of the trees' ceremonial importance, chewing through their trunks, dragging them off, and heaping them all together into a mass grave, a great memorial dam.

Alta didn't want anything to grow in her name after she died. She wanted a hole to open up and swallow her, and maybe a nice-looking man or two. The pair assigned to her table were no good, but there were other men at In the Pines, who were handsome and seemed warmish and alert. She had a habit of making quick, stubborn judgments, and maybe her perception had slipped a little, because lately, whenever she made up her mind to talk to a man, he'd say something like "I miss my car," or "Noodles are all I can stomach these days."

Once she took pride in her perception. Now it was punishing her. Once she was confident of the effect she had on others. Now it was as if her fellow tenants were suffering her like a chill, waiting for her to go away.

•

Alta first saw the soldier from her back patio, swatting at the high grass with his saber in the early afternoon. The field was shrill with sunlight. She watched and might have happily continued to watch as he walked on past, creeping far off into her view, briefly residing in it, then moving on. She might've noticed him without noting him, like the elapsing of a memory left untended. But when the soldier saw Alta sitting on her patio, he halted, smiled, and began swatting a path toward her.

He reached the edge of the field, took off his hat, and said, "Permission to come aboard." Two more steps until

Alta's patio. He was an older man, with orderly features and a waffled sunburned neck. His blue felt jacket was dark at the armpits.

"Are you lost?" Alta asked.

"I was," he said. "My men are camped up on some ridge a ways back, singing beautiful songs about liberty and transformation. I set out to look for some berries and mushrooms and things. We're hurting for rations."

She invited him to sit. He sheathed his saber and sighed before dropping himself into the plastic chair. He was in his late fifties, maybe, no watch, no wedding band. He scanned the fields slowly, stopping when his gaze reached the phone tower. "Sometimes you're watching the world," he said, "and the world's watching right back."

As he said this, Alta looked down at herself and saw that she was wearing her yellow bathrobe over her clothes, which she often did, to keep warm. She couldn't recall changing into the bathrobe, but there it was, indisputably on her. She practiced a few responses, then said, "And sometimes you fall asleep but don't realize it until you wake up with a man on your patio."

The soldier smiled. "Well put," he said, extending a hand to Alta. "Lieutenant Charles Thorn." She shook his big, warm hand and introduced herself and together they watched the flat grass retreat and advance and retreat. Alta waited for him to explain the uniform, what he was actually doing in the field, anything. But she was neither uncomfortable nor overly curious about it. She could still feel his warmth on her hand.

The lieutenant let out a tidy, satisfied sigh. "You're brave," he said finally. "Staying out here while the war rambles through." He crossed and uncrossed his arms. "You probably have a husband or sons or some loved ones fighting?"

Alta started to say no but hesitated. The question wasn't a question, but an opening, an invitation. "Come to think of it," she said, "I bet I do. Any news?"

"Sporadic. So far it's just some cavalry making raids on the fringes, rummaging, pillaging what they can." The lieutenant turned around in his chair and looked through the patio door into Alta's apartment. "This place looks solidly fortified but you never know. Are there any other women in there?"

"Just us active seniors," Alta said. "Maybe a few nurses, none too appealing."

"You'd be shocked," the lieutenant said, "at what appeals to them. We're talking about men who have amorous interactions with horses and dogs and livestock and each other and trees, even, whatever's softest and available." He shook his head so vigorously his brass buttons rattled. "Sorry. I haven't talked to a woman in a few months. I've forgotten how."

"You're doing fine," Alta said. "Tell me about the war."

And the lieutenant did. He told her about his battalion, a group of men from western Massachusetts, and about the little skirmishes and larger battles they'd seen so far. He was a deadpan storyteller, dotting his account with words like *contretemps, sanguinary, asunder.* He used his hands to shape what he described and paused after anything solemn: "At night in the encampments you can hear men crying in their sleep. Crying because no matter what they've done up until now, no matter how grand their aspirations, they've all been funneled to exactly the same god-awful place."

Alta let herself settle into the cozy tragedy of it all. There was a kinship, because she, too, felt as if she'd been funneled to a place to join a company of people who neither cared about nor comforted her. Her routine had been permanently inter-rupted. Her past had been torn from her future and now here she was, subsisting on the bleak, ripped brim of the present. She didn't even have a dining room anymore.

Before the lieutenant left, he reached into his jacket and presented her with a dried-out seedpod he'd found while searching for food. "It's extremely valuable," he said. "I'm giving it to you for safekeeping, and so I have a reason to come back."

He put on his hat and ran his hand over the front of his jacket, which was adorned with—Alta counted them—seven long black bars. One for each day of the week. He took her hand, leaned down, and kissed it with his chapped lips. The saber's blade, Alta could see, was engraved with something, but it was too faint for her to decipher.

She followed his outline as it wended through the field, swatting the grass with the saber, then disappearing over a small hill.

The moment he was gone, she wondered when he would return. She imagined him lying wounded on the battlefield gripping his stomach in agony, waiting for someone to cart him off. The image remained while she went inside to get ready for dinner until, after a while, it yielded to another image: Vic, her first husband, crouching in the backyard, irately pulling weeds. He was most entertaining when angry, and yard work made him angry, so Alta sometimes watched him from the kitchen window. One afternoon, she looked out to see him straining near the little camphor tree, banging his fist against his chest. She first thought maybe he was mad at the tree, or at her, but he was actually dying of a heart attack, a *substantial* heart attack, the doctor would later tell her. He was trying to punch himself back to life.

After dinner, she returned to her apartment in a good mood, and found a blank notepad. She brought it to the dining-room table, opened it, and wrote on the first blank page: *Here's all I know about men.*

She'd had the idea at dinner to make a list for herself, to use it to organize her mind. She thought, *Men are sometimes . . . tall. Men like certain . . . things.* But she was too tired to remember them, both the things and the men. She underlined the one sentence, to make it look more imperative for her to return to it, and put it away.

A few days later, Alta sat on her patio after breakfast. Several times the high grass parted in such a way that she was sure someone would emerge, but the grass blew the other way and the horizon returned to ordinary. Alta ate a too-soft banana and flung the peel into the field when she was finished. "Damn this sundered country," Alta said, and laughed. "Damn this Civil War." She laughed until she made herself cough and then she stopped.

A blackbird circled and went call call call. The red beacon light atop the phone tower pulsed like a machine heart.

The lieutenant had better hurry: she wouldn't wait all day. She was alone, yes, but she wasn't *that* lonely. She could always walk over to her next-door neighbor's, a not-bad-looking ex-optician named Fenn, and knock on his sliding glass door. Tell him she was locked out of her apartment, or that she needed to borrow a hammer, needed him to turn down his television, comb his hair, and whisper something tender into her ear . . .

Fenn, though, was out of the running. He'd hung a flag on his patio that said SPRING HAS SPRUNG and which featured two bunnies chewing carrots, and he watched game shows at maximum volume all day long. Sometimes she'd hear his voice through the wall, and think he had a visitor, but it would turn out that it was just Fenn guessing along with the contestants. The viola! Marvin Hagler! Brussels!

There was no shame in waiting for the lieutenant. He

would either arrive or he wouldn't. If he arrived, she would invite him in for a drink. ("If it isn't too much trouble," he'd say. "Don't be silly," she'd say. "You look like you need one.") She came up with about a dozen different throwaway greetings: Come aboard; Hark; It's about time; You look thirsty; Hello again; How's the war; Don't hurt me, I'm unarmed . . .

She continued sitting on her patio, watching the overgrown grass flit and shimmy to reveal flashes of pale, scalplike earth. No shame in watching the overgrown grass flit and shimmy.

Later, after dinner, the wind calmed down and she saw the lieutenant in the distance, chopping at the air with his saber. He was wearing a cleaner uniform shirt, one with a second row of buttons and gold piping along the sleeves. His saber glinted with fierce aluminum light until he sheathed it.

"I come with news," he said, huffing into the empty chair next to Alta, "of unquestionable badness." He didn't wait for a reply. "Things are heating up. Two Confederate regiments are on their way here right now, to join the two that've already arrived. You can't stay here. You need to leave while it's still quiet."

"Too late for that," Alta said. "I don't have anywhere to go."

"Nowhere? No family or friends in nearby towns?"

"I've been relocated for the last time."

His eyes wandered and stuttered across Alta's face.

"Life," he said, and sighed. She thought he was going to pursue this further, but that was all he said. Alta was excited by the imminence of the enemy and by the lieutenant's heavy breathing, which seemed to parallel each other and coiled into Alta's mind. The day was warmly lucid and soon there'd be horses galloping to the sound of artillery and drums. How gallant everyone would be, weeping as they fired at the enemy, figuring out how best to describe the bleak night wind in their next letter home. Alta said, "Have you heard any news of my men?"

"They're in Buford's outfit, right?"

"Buford, yes. Those are the ones."

The lieutenant nodded. "That's the reason I'm here, actually." He crossed and uncrossed his arms with a crackling of joints. "They were captured, Alta. Yesterday. They were undermanned, caught out in the open, and they got snagged. Could be good news for them. They're done fighting for a while. They probably have a better chance of survival."

"Men," Alta said. "You make promises you can't keep, and keep promises you never made. You create a lot of noise but it adds up to barely a sneeze."

She saw from the lieutenant's reaction that this was a fine, an agreeable retort. He put his hand on her leg and the weight of it made her feel like something he could handily dispatch. She didn't mind the feeling.

"I've got another precious trinket I'd like you to look after." He unfastened the middle button on his jacket and reached in for an enormous ebony-colored nut. "It's heirloom-grade," he said. "Very rare. I trust you'll know how to care for it."

She took it from him and ran her fingers over the smooth outer shell. Briefly she had the urge to shout, "It's just a nut!" and burn away the pretense of the game they were playing, but the urge passed, and she let it. "This means you'll be back?"

The lieutenant stood up. "I promise," he said, smiling. He saluted her with two fingers, unsheathed his saber, said, "Onward!" and was off.

Later on, she heard cannon fire in the distance. It was a festive, unthreatening sound. As it moved closer and boomed louder, she tried to locate it on the battlefield, beyond the high grass. But it turned out that the sound was coming from behind her, on the other side of the apartment building. Closer, another boom, an accompanying hiss, and then the sound of wheels on asphalt as the garbage truck advanced north to grab another Dumpster.

•

Alta was among the war-wounded and war-weary. They huddled over puzzle pieces in the activity room, turning them over one by one. "Border first," Fenn was saying. "Inside last." The puzzle was a picture of a lake at dawn, colorful sailboats rigged to a dock. Alta watched the puzzle come together in clusters, first the border, then the boats, then the water, then the sky. Everyone gasped hungrily from barely agape mouths.

She left before the puzzle was finished. She followed the vacuum stroke marks down the hallway carpet, which was the same nerve-racking palm-leaf pattern as the carpet in her apartment. The vacuum marks usually led her to the cafeteria, but today they veered left into the multipurpose room, and so did she. The room was brightly lit and filled with residents sitting in rows. Onstage, holding a microphone, was Mr. Santos, the head of In the Pines. Bald, red-faced, and thin, he reminded Alta of a talking digestive organ. Standing next to him were four little girls in hoop dresses.

"What would you like us to know about you?" Mr. Santos asked one of them. He pointed the microphone toward the girl and she said, "I love my school."

"And what do you love about it?" Mr. Santos asked.

The girl, who couldn't have been older than six, thought about it for a moment, then said, "Everything." Mr. Santos nodded his bald head and said to the crowd, "Was that delightful? I thought it was delightful."

Alta sat down next to a friendly-looking man in a wheelchair. He was making notes on a card with a pencil stub.

"What is this?" Alta asked him. "What are you doing?"

"Keeping score," he said. "Little brown-hair's completely stealing the show. She's incredible. They still have scorecards if you need one."

"I'm half Canadian," a blond-haired girl was saying. "I

love the winter. I have a snow globe on my shelf that I look at all year and I wish I was tiny enough to live inside it."

"Aww," said Mr. Santos and some of the residents in the audience.

"Okay," the man in the wheelchair said, shaking his head. "That was rehearsed."

Alta needed to leave—in her mind she was already following the vacuum marks back to her apartment—but she couldn't seem to stand up. Every so often she said to the man in the wheelchair, "I need to hurry along soon." She watched as each of the young girls sang a song, then talked about how much her grandparents meant to her. Alta wanted to root for a specific girl, but whenever one of them spoke Alta changed her mind. There was something unbearably alive in each of them, alive and rash and scrambling for egress.

Alta felt the same way. She had lain in bed these past few nights, unable to sleep, ears still ringing from the noise of the day. The sound of voices placed atop one another like letters in a mailbox, and atop all of them the lieutenant's. A big, good voice with a theatrical undertow to make it clear he was playing a game. She'd placed the seedpod and the nut on her kitchen windowsill so she could study them while she washed her hands. She knew neither the lieutenant's intent nor her own, but she knew the rules of the game, and for the moment, certainly for now, this was plenty.

Before she'd left her apartment, she taped a note to her patio door, which said I WILL RETURN ANON. She liked the word *anon*. Like a powdered veil, it provided cover for the fear that the lieutenant wasn't coming back. Sitting next to the man in the wheelchair, she said, "I need to leave. I have a good friend, a soldier, who's stopping by. I hate to keep people waiting."

The man in the wheelchair let out a harried little sigh. "Hand job," he announced. "That's probably all he's going to have time for."

Alta had never heard this word before, yet she knew immediately what it meant. She studied him, trying to gauge by his expression what his intent was. He looked aggressively satisfied. "That wasn't necessary," she said. "You might've given up but some haven't. I haven't."

"I'm only teasing you," the man said as Alta stood up to leave. "I bet your soldier has time for all of it."

"You shouldn't be allowed around children," Alta told him. "You should try to maybe show a little more . . . valor."

The man in the wheelchair laughed at his scorecard. "Valor," he repeated. "Valor's how I ended up in this goddamn thing. From now on it's sniping and petty malice."

In her apartment, Alta microwaved a freezer pretzel and brought it in a napkin to the patio. She pulled down the note and saw beneath her message, scribbled in faint pencil letters: ENEMY SIGHTED. BATTLE IMMINENT. PRAY FOR OUR MEN.

On the arm of her patio chair was a red oval leaf. She brought it inside, placed it on the kitchen windowsill beside the others.

The wind made barely a sound, Alta realized. Whatever was strained and blown by it—leaves, grass, scarves, flags—did the work. The gusts called to mind a neglected house, a storm door opening and closing, opening and closing.

Everyone made a noise. Her first husband made a glassy noise. Her second and third made humming and rasping noises, respectively. Thinking about the husbands reminded her of the lieutenant, and remembering the lieutenant, who made the most noise of all—a marching-away noise—now reminded her of the man in the wheelchair. Who made a word noise: *Hand job.* From time to time she still waited for the lieutenant on her patio, and this wasn't reasonable, she knew, but who expected her to be reasonable with so much noise?

The Boer War! Fenn yelled through the wall. *Geometry!*

Far away, the battle made a faraway garbage-truck noise. Her men were there. She'd dreamed about them, Vic, Don, George, all charging the enemy with the same rifle. Acting and counteracting.

She awoke thinking: *I am losing my mind.* She'd begun saying this aloud before George died. Whenever she couldn't find her keys, or when she forgot to turn off the television. She wanted to get into the habit of saying it so that she'd remember to continue to once she indeed started losing her mind. Saying it aloud, even if it didn't avert things, might at least soften the stupor when it came. Make her sympathetic, the same way a drunk admitting he was drunk lent himself a sorry sort of dignity.

One night, after reading a magazine article about how the brain like any other muscle needed regular exercise, she told George she wanted him to start asking her more questions. This was one of the suggestions in the article.

"About what?" he'd asked. They were in the living room, having a predinner drink. Alta drank a glass of sherry while George sipped an unrefrigerated Coors from its twinkly can.

"Anything," she said.

He squinted, considering. Though not handsome, his face had a volatile softness that made it interesting to look at. "Name me," he said, looking at his beer can. "I'm what you get by combining copper and tin."

Watching him wait for the answer, she tried to remember what it was he'd first said to her, how he'd expressed interest. It wasn't much. *Hello*, maybe. Or, *Hey you*. After Vic she stayed a widow for a few years, but Don came along and then George, and here she was, sitting next to her third husband, her *third*, a couple of spent batteries nestled inside a toy. George sighed while Alta listened. She knew she'd outlive him. She could hear his spirit clawing off as he breathed.

When you combined copper and tin, you got . . . something else. "I have no idea," she said.

"Uh-oh."

"What?"

He patted at his shirt with a napkin. "Spilled a little beer."

He was going to make her ask for the answer. Though she knew very little about him, she knew him. She knew that he would continue silently sipping his room-warm Coors until she said something.

"Out with it," she said. "What do you get?"

One final sip. "I am bronze," he said. "I am the world's first alloy."

She liked thinking of her men out on the battlefield with the lieutenant. It gave her a tighter stage on which to regard them all. George the last, Don the middle, Vic the first. Vic, who made himself known to her in high school by using masking tape to make a line from his front door, down the sidewalk, around the corner, down another sidewalk, all the way to Alta's house. He was in some of her classes but she'd never noticed him before; after this, she couldn't quit noticing him. He had pale hands and he held his pencil like a fork, poised for when the teacher said something noteworthy. He sneezed and, when Alta said bless you, he nodded. Alta perceived everything about him in that sneeze and nod.

After Vic came Don, then George. Each damaged her fortifications a little, made the next one possible. Sometimes, waiting on her patio for the lieutenant, she felt as if she'd squandered her affection. She had exchanged it for a few shared meals and a shoebox of photographs. Not long after they died, the circuit failed and she was getting married again, and again. Thinking about them now, Vic and Don and George, they were easily drowned out by the advance and retreat, the rustle and thump, of the wind. Where was the lieutenant?

She brought weird-smelling apples and overripe bananas onto the patio and ate them there, throwing the core or the peel into the field when she was done with it. She waited for news. Just when she thought she'd sufficiently lost hope of the lieutenant returning, she saw a distant movement in the grass, a glint of dark color—she would sit up in her chair, crane her neck, and find there was a little more hope to lose.

Sometimes the fruit would get hung up in the high grass, where she could watch them tan and wither for the next few days.

"Casualties," she'd say when that happened. She might forget where she was, or when it was, but never for long. *There are no new wars*, she'd think, and then she'd think the opposite, *There are only new wars*, and that seemed true as well. She sensed she was growing smaller and smaller, that her own noise was becoming shallower, a murmur.

•

Brenna, Alta's great-niece, called one afternoon and asked how she was doing. Fine, Alta told her. She asked if Alta would mind if she came over sometime and Alta said no, and a few minutes later there was a knock at the door. She'd been calling from the lobby.

"I won't stay long," she said before sitting down on the

sofa. Brenna had a flushed, pretty, complex face that made her look as if she spoke a different language. "I love what you've done with the place."

Alta looked around. She hadn't done anything except hang a portrait of a peach-colored seascape that Don had painted. She offered Brenna a cup of coffee and, when Brenna accepted, remembered she no longer had a coffeemaker. She went into the kitchen, microwaved a mug of water, and dropped a tea bag into it.

"It's nice knowing you're nearby," Brenna said, sipping the tea. "I have such nice memories of you in Florida. The beach. Uncle Vic taking us to look at all the jellyfish that had washed ashore. The man-of-wars with the purple tentacles. You remember?"

Alta remembered. She remembered Vic liked making up stories about the jellyfish, telling the kids that they were from a different planet, that once high tide pulled them back out to sea, they would find their mother ship and go home.

"Men-of-war," Alta said.

Brenna had been an odd child. When she came to visit Alta and Vic, she would sleep in a sleeping bag on top of the covers, because she didn't like the feel of the sheets on her legs. She was a hoarder, too. She stockpiled candy and pocket change, and if you asked her what she planned to do with it, she would say, she couldn't have been older than nine, she'd say: "Have it." She planned to have it.

Brenna said to Alta: "I'm getting married."

"Well," Alta said, studying the girl on the sofa, trying to calculate what this had to do with her memory of the girl. "That's good news. I met a man, too. I met him behind my apartment."

Brenna stood up and walked over to Alta in her chair and hugged her. "I'm so happy for you, Aunt Alta. I love how everything's worked out."

Alta had to lean forward to accept the hug, and when she did, her hand landed on the girl's backbone and she smelled a crushed-rose fragrance in her hair. The girl sat back on the sofa, straightened her skirt, and said she wanted to ask Alta for a favor. Her face became less animated, dumber. She said, "I was hoping you'd let me have your wedding ring. The one your grandmother gave you."

Alta smelled the crushed-rose smell and still heard the girl's assessment: *Everything's worked out.* The girl was so young. She thought love was a door you carefully opened once, just once, and then you were there. Where? It didn't matter. Opening the door was the important part, making sure you locked it once you were through, and maybe the reason Alta loved Vic then Don then George was because she never thought to lock the door. She gazed at her apartment key on the metal hook and fought the urge to get up and lock the front door.

"I don't want to impose," Brenna said. "I bet it still means a lot to you. I just want you to know I'd be honored to wear it."

She'd be honored to wear Alta's *key*? Alta hesitated for a few seconds and then remembered that Brenna had asked about the wedding ring. She looked so earnest and inflated with anticipation. *I'd be honored* was rehearsed, which, more than anything, made Alta not want to give her the ring. But it was only a momentary impulse, an itch that Alta could ignore. Besides, she didn't need the ring anymore.

"Wait here," she said to Brenna, and she went into her bedroom and opened up her jewelry box for the first time since moving to In the Pines. She found her engagement ring, two twisted gold bands studded with pallid gemstones.

When Alta brought the ring to the girl, she was smoothing the front of her skirt. She took the ring and, her eyes beginning to tear up, brought it to her face, her mouth opening slightly. "Don't eat it," Alta said.

"I am so grateful," Brenna said. Then, studying the ring, hesitating, looking pained: "I don't think it's the right one. Katie said it was silver, with sapphires along it?"

Alta looked at the ring and realized that this was the one Don had given her. He'd offered it to her at night while they were walking his dog. Don had picked a flower from a magnolia tree, given it to her, and asked her to marry him. All the way home he hummed an unidentifiable song: *hmm-hmm-hmm, hmm-hmm, hmm-hmm-hmm-hmm.*

When Alta brought out the correct ring, Brenna stood and said, with slightly diminished emotion, "I am so grateful." She reached into her purse, pulled out a beige engraved envelope, and set it on the coffee table. She waited with a smile. Alta realized that this was the kind of moment when she was expected to say something vast and benevolent to solidify the exchange.

"Save a little of yourself," she said to the girl. "Just a little. He'll never miss it."

The girl nodded, as if to a song whose words she didn't know, steadily. "That's really wise," she said. "That means a lot, for you to pass that along."

"I don't think it's all that wise," Alta said. "It just took me a long time to figure it out."

"But still," the girl said.

Afterward, sitting on her patio, Alta knew she could've told Brenna to eat corn chowder only on odd-numbered Thursdays and the girl would've said that means a lot. She, Brenna, wasn't going to dwell on anything that might muddy her happiness. From now on she was going to gather it up, hoard it, and keep it clean.

"I'm going to sit on my patio to enjoy my view," Alta had said to her. "If you want, you can join me."

"I'd love to," the girl said. But she couldn't. She needed to go tell everyone the good news. She had brought an empty gray ring box with a plush little slit in which she secured the ring. The box made a croaking sound when she closed it, a swallowing-up sound.

Alta was a lifeguard. She sat on her back patio and scanned the grass for problem areas, never looking at the same spot for too long. She wasn't sure what she was guarding, but when the wind blew through, she could see banana peels and fruit cores in the low grass. Stray cats came through, birds, owls, foxes maybe, possums maybe, raccoons, squirrels, snakes, men.

Once, a pair of men with metal detectors and shovels wandered in and Alta watched as they slowly passed through, stopping every so often to dig. A different version of Alta might consider wading out into the grass and leaving a trail of coins to her patio door for the next metal detectors to come find. Taping a note on her sliding glass door that said: BETTER TREASURE INSIDE.

This would involve a major refashioning. Leaving a note like that meant fashioning herself into the sort of woman who would leave a note like that. A woman who wore scarves and costume jewelry. Who calmly told men, when they made mention of hand jobs, to go choke on a vitamin.

One afternoon, someone came up from behind her while she was on her patio and tapped a hand on her shoulder, trying to surprise her.

"Oh," Alta said. It was the lieutenant, wearing not his hat and uniform but a pair of ironed chinos and a new-looking pearl-button shirt. His hair was sandy-gray. He looked older though somehow sturdier without the uniform. "You could scare a person like that."

"Mind if I sit down?" he asked.

No, Alta didn't mind. She never minded, not once.

The lieutenant sat in the other chair and folded his hands in his lap. He smiled, hesitated, smiled again, as if crossing and uncrossing things off a list. "Well, war's over," he said. "We won."

"I heard," Alta said. "It was in all the newspapers."

"Now comes Reconstruction."

"Then another war."

"It never ends," he said.

"I'm glad you came back," she said.

She went inside and returned with two scotches and water, then went inside again and came back out with all the items he'd left on her patio. He sipped the scotch and talked about his days as a history teacher. There was a new earnestness to his voice, a cleaner pitch. He told her about a sign he'd hung next to the clock in his classroom, which said TIME PASSES, WILL YOU? It was meant to scare students into concentrating, but it probably had the opposite effect, like most of what he did in the classroom.

"How about you," he said after a while. "You seem to be out here on your patio a good bit. Are you a bird-watcher?"

A fine question, which Alta thought about while gazing at the field. The night before was cold and she had dreamed she was making a quilt out of Vic, Don, George, and the lieutenant, sewing their legs and chests together while telling them to remain very still.

"Maybe," she said.

"Maybe? You aren't sure?"

A few seconds later, a crow landed near the edge of her yard, hunted around in the grass, and found a shriveled apple core. It picked up and dropped the core several times, trying to better its purchase. Two flaps of its wings and the crow was up, off.

"I wasn't," Alta said. "Not until now."

first marriage

They noticed the odor outside Tucson the day
after they got married. They were driving on a bleak
stretch of highway and Tad thought they might be
near a rendering plant or a dead coyote, but twenty
miles later the odor hadn't dissipated. It was putrid
and dense and seemed to be getting denser. Amy
drove with her hand over her nose while Tad rolled
down the windows and breathed.

"Don't worry," he said. "We're not far."

They were headed to Bisbee in a car, a Volvo, that belonged to a man named Gar Floyd, who expected them in Jacksonville, Florida, in eight days. This was their destination or, more accurately, their halfway point. The car was part of a program called Drive Way. In Florida they'd be given somebody else's car, which they would drive back to California.

"It's thickening on my tongue," Amy said. "It's like we're being punished."

The odor swelled. It ate at the air. It was as if some giant, blood-rancid bird had dragged itself into the backseat and spread its wings and roosted there.

•

In Bisbee the station attendant sat in the driver's seat and closed his eyes. A few seconds later, he stepped out of the car, coughed, wiped his hands on a blue towel, coughed again, and said, "It's animal."

Tad and Amy looked at each other. Amy handed over the keys and she and Tad walked their luggage to their motel: a cluster of Airstream trailers decorated with atomic-print throw pillows and chintz curtains. Theirs was the Royal Manor. Tad rifled through the cabinets while Amy showered. He found an old saltine tin filled with condoms, a drawer of taped radio shows from the fifties. He found a book labeled GUEST MEMORIES. He looked through it, the road still humming under him. *Cactus wrens in the old cemetery. The shrine at dawn. Oni made her special beans!*

He found a pen. *Today's the second day of our first marriage*, he wrote. *We have no special beans, but we've tasted victory and defeat and both were wonderful.*

The last part was something he'd read in a book about the Civil War. It used to be his slogan, when he had a slogan. Now he had no slogan. He listened to Amy mashing shampoo into her hair. He felt consigned and content and resigned. He fished one of the condoms out of the tin, undressed, and got under the covers. He felt like a costume waiting to be worn, an odd feeling but not at all disagreeable, not at all.

●

They climbed a rounded bluff to see the shrine, built by a father to his son. There were plastic carnations and school pictures of a smiling black-haired boy. On the east-facing side of the shrine the pictures had faded to beige in the sun. The shrine seemed cheap, disused. Noticing a shelf for offerings, Tad searched his wallet and found a punch card from the Sub Hut, which he parted with. "Enshrined," he said. He lifted the collar of his shirt and smelled it. It smelled like shirt.

He looked over the town: laundry lines and kiddie pools and satellite dishes mounted to roofs and trained to the same remote object. Farther on, the copper pit, cactus and scrub, barrenness.

He sat down, closed his eyes, and listened to the click-and-advance of Amy's disposable camera. She'd been taking pictures since they left, gathering evidence of their good time. She was sentimental, discreetly. She saved birthday cards. She couldn't pass a Missing Pet sign without noting how tragic the child's handwriting was. Sometimes when Tad looked at her he saw someone stronger, more permanent and at ease with herself than he would ever be. And other times he saw something less certain, a question unanswered, a teetering pile of wishes . . .

When he opened his eyes, she was scrutinizing the camera. "Won't zoom," she said. The abrupt way she spoke made it sound German. "Hey, maybe they'll take our picture."

A middle-aged couple in khaki shorts and fanny packs approached, their voices seeming to speed up as they neared. The man said, "The clerk at the hotel keeps saying, 'I'd eat the streets. I'd *eat* the streets.' He's trying to say the streets are clean."

The woman accepted the camera from Amy. She held it to her face and counted, her top lip quivering like a dreaming dog's, *three, two, one.*

"We got married this morning," Tad said after she returned the camera. "This is our honeymoon."

"How wonderful," the woman said. She surveyed her husband until his truculent expression softened.

"I just realized I left the bouquet in the car," Amy said. She put her hand to her face tentatively. "It's probably ruined."

"We can pick another one," Tad said.

"No. Are you serious?"

He supposed he was. Unthinking, but serious, he supposed. "Of course I'm not serious."

Amy watched him with puzzled amusement. She watched him like a child waiting for a top to spin itself out.

"We're so in love," Tad said to the couple, "we could fall off this bluff and it wouldn't be tragic. It'd be romantic."

"Poetry," the woman said.

"Horseshit," the man mumbled.

There seemed nothing else to say. Tad noticed the couple was dressed identically except for their fanny packs, which were as unalike as could be. This heartened him, the fact that they'd been unable to coordinate the fanny packs.

"Speaking of which," the man said. "I believe one of us stepped in some." They lifted their feet to check. Tad smelled his shirt again, a mixture of fabric and fabric softener. "Don't let Frank ruin your moment," the woman said.

•

Back in the trailer, Amy lay down and Tad put in a radio show called "No One Left." A man wakes to find that everyone has disappeared. At first the man, who lives alone and despises his neighbors, is thrilled. He goes to the beach, takes what he wants from stores. But soon he's lonely. Six months later, he's raving in the streets. "I can't do it anymore!" he says. "I need to be seen!" He goes into a pharmacy and swallows a handful of sleeping pills. Just as he does, a pay phone rings, rings again, again.

"What a cruel turn," Amy said.

"It was probably just a telemarketer."

She sighed, exasperated. "You're always saying things like that. Clever, insignificant things."

This seemed excessively bitter, but he let it pass. Besides, she was right. She was almost always right. Recognizing this and conceding to it allowed him a little dignity, he hoped.

She sat up and rubbed lotion onto her shins. She'd packed a battery of lotions to fight the desert air, a lotion for each body part. Tad began kissing her stomach, arms, legs, neck, stopping to smell the different lotions. It was like a theme park, where you could visit eight countries in a single day.

"Are we really married?" she asked.

He held out his hand to show her the thin band of turquoise they'd bought at a souvenir shop near the courthouse.

"I mean, I'm still figuring out how to feel about it. I used to think it'd be like getting my ears pierced. Only, I don't know. More."

"Don't try so hard," he said. "Let's enjoy our honeymoon. We can always get divorced on the way home."

"That's what I mean! You keep doing that, diminishing it. Acting like it's nothing special."

"Finding each other was special, but we've been together

three years. Getting married's just confetti after the party."

"We should at least pretend."

Tad felt like he was being led through a series of increasingly smaller doors. "Okay, let's pretend. Let's talk about all the things we'll do."

"Sometimes it's like you're talking underwater." With her thumbnail she scraped at the skin on her knee, then studied the results unfondly. "I mean, I know you're doing your best."

"I always do my best," he said quickly. Then, "What do you mean?"

"I don't know. I'm beat. I'm married."

"Confetti," he said. "Come here."

She acquiesced. Her body was warm, moist, and unsurprising. Tad closed his eyes and pretended they were trapped on a Ferris wheel. It was their first date and they were nervous and then the Ferris wheel stopped. They held hands and soon began kissing and taking off each other's clothes. Tad imagined the Ferris wheel starting up again and spinning faster. Their trailer seemed to buck and sway, in tune with the scenario. Their inhibitions were brittle, they flaked off like skin.

•

They'd gotten married the day before in Lake Havasu City. Lake Havasu City was the Home of the London Bridge, the billboards said, but they must have driven past it or across it without realizing it. They parked in front of the courthouse, went inside, and took a number.

Tad, wearing eel-skin boots and a bolo tie, looked like the brother of somebody famous. The judge asked him if he was in the military; it seemed like he was in a hurry, the judge said. The bailiff took pictures with Amy's disposable camera. Afterward he handed her a bag of sample-size dish soaps and detergents, FOR A FRESH HOUSEHOLD, the label said.

She drove while Tad read the owner's manual and re-programmed the radio stations every hour or so. It felt good to be logging miles, to command something so imperative. They discussed Gar Floyd's likes and dislikes. Gar Floyd liked raggedy women, they decided. Gar Floyd did not like the idea of milking a goat. The rear armrest folded down to reveal an oval opening to the trunk and Tad and Amy tried to guess its purpose before Tad looked it up in the owner's manual. "Snow skis," he told her.

They'd guessed it was where Gar Floyd stowed open beers when the police pulled him over. An airhole in case Gar Floyd was trapped in the trunk.

"Our first marriage," Tad kept saying as they drove south toward Phoenix. They passed cinder-red rocks. Saguaro cactuses shaped like people being robbed. The wildflowers he picked for her bouquet were drying on the dashboard. "What are you thinking about?" he asked her.

"You," she said. "Me. You and me." She was wearing the white linen sundress she'd bought for the ceremony. She looked drugged, lovely. "I'm trying to decide what sort of life we're going to have."

"Uh-oh," he said. He reached over to her with an imaginary microphone. "What kind of life are you deciding to have?"

"I can't say really. It's more like a hue, a general mood."

"What kind of mood?"

She peeked down at Tad's hand next to her chin. "Unfamiliar," she said.

Parked between two snoring semis at a highway rest stop, they had sex in the backseat of the Volvo. They planned to do this in every state they crossed. Sex in Gar Floyd's car was a wonderful novelty, like life itself. Back on the highway, they passed a Tercel with blinking hazard lights and JUST MARRIED soaped on its back window. Amy honked the horn, Tad waved. Behind the wheel was a bearded man in a tuxedo, and next to him, a woman in a peach-colored dress.

Tad thought, *Right here, this moment, no before, no after.* He couldn't recall where he'd heard it. It was either from a philosophy book or an aerobics video. He felt a fierce contentment. He wished there was a way to ration it out to make it last longer. But there was no way. It ignited, it burned up, it was gone.

The man in the tuxedo lifted a can of Schlitz and toasted them as they drove past.

The Volvo sat in the garage, a fan perched atop a toolbox blowing into the open door. Tad approached the car and, leaning in, sniffed. The odor reached out like a slap, sharp and undiminished. It smelled to Tad like *membrane* or *groats*, not the things but the words.

"At first we thought it was on the engine block," the mechanic said. "It happens, with kitties especially. They crawl up there to get warm. When you start the car, the fan belt just annihilates them. You would've noticed that." He seemed pleased with his story so far. The odor still reached Tad from where he stood, or else it'd stayed in his nose.

"It was a snake, from the looks of it," he continued. "Probably went in through your wheel well and couldn't get out. Starved. We pulled the backseat and there it was. Little old coral snake."

The mechanic paused while the office door creaked open and a black dog trotted out, followed by an elderly man in spotless coveralls. The spotlessness of his uniform seemed proof that he was in charge. The dog lay down the instant he stopped walking. "It's a shame," the man said. "It was a nice car."

"Was?" Tad said, adding, "It's not our car." He looked at his watch. The minute hand pointed to one number, the hour hand to another. "We need to be in Florida in eight days."

The old man laughed noiselessly. "You're just about through with Arizona. All that's left is New Mexico, Texas, a few others. What takes you to Florida?"

"I don't know, what takes you to Florida?"

"I'm asking you. People often have reasons for going to Florida."

"Oh," Tad said. "The way you said it, I thought it was a joke."

The old man laughed again. Just his shoulders shook. "It's no joke, son. It's a goddamn predicament!" The dog perked up when the man raised his voice, and the man patted him softly. "We'll keep air on it, but it takes time. Right now it's a scream. Might be down to a yelp tomorrow. Didn't you say you're on your honeymoon?"

Tad nodded. He was looking into the car at the bouquet, still drying on the dashboard, remembering something before he retrieved it.

"Why are we talking about snakes then? If I were you I'd be celebrating. Hell, I'd be back at your motel having fun. What do you say, Jeff?"

Tad waited for the other mechanic to say something, but it turned out that Jeff was the dog. Jeff didn't say anything. "This is ridiculous," Tad said. "Can't you do anything else? This car belongs to a very impatient man."

The old man scratched his shoulder. Where his neck met his clavicle, Tad noticed one of those flesh-colored nicotine patches that always made him a little sick to his stomach.

"Sure we can," the mechanic said. And then to the other man: "Go in my office and grab that other fan."

After hesitating to look at the bouquet once more, Tad left.

He bought a six-pack of beer and walked back to the trailer as the sun set. The horizon was violently radiant and the wind sung with borrowed nostalgia. It was growing colder. He passed the immense copper pit, a fenced-off canyon of wrecked earth at least a half-mile across, staircased and very still. Tad peered through the fence. The damage looked cataclysmic up close, but seen from space it was nothing. Seen from space it didn't amount to a pinprick. This struck him as a nice, comprehensive thing to realize. He wanted to realize more things like it, but it was getting too cold to concentrate. On the road again, he decided that if anybody asked what he was doing, he'd say, very casually, "Just passing through." But no one did.

In grade school, he used to pretend to chew gum in class. When the teacher asked him to spit it out, he would pretend to swallow it. This was what he remembered while he looked at the bouquet. The old man reminded him of the teacher, something about how he lazily regulated the conversation.

In the trailer, Amy sat on the edge of the bed, her head pitched forward slightly on her long neck, as it did when she was unsure of something. He came closer and she said, "Tad." The word released a smell like sweet dough. "We aren't moving, are we? It feels like we're being pulled behind a truck."

He told her about the snake and waited while his disappointment became their disappointment. "That's so awful," she said. Tad's impulse was to make her feel better, and why not? There were a hundred ways to make her feel better, a hundred possibilities. But as he stared at the white underside of the comforter, scorched with an iron mark, he was dim with hesitation.

She said, "I was remembering when I was little, how I'd lie naked in bed after a shower. I'd feel this amazing . . . *thing* happening inside me. This event. Like my body was just the thinnest husk to hide what was going on inside. I'd try to imagine what my husband would be like, what he was doing at that very moment."

"Probably thinking about girls like you, naked in their beds."

"I hope not. I was nine."

"Maybe I was riding my bike. Was it summer?"

"I imagined him traveling a great distance, suffering setbacks."

"A hero, earning his way to you."

She closed her eyes and smiled. Her face looked slightly misshapen. Was something happening inside her? He waited for her face to show signs of relief. He was distracted by the sound of a coyote. *Ah-oooooo.* So faint and wavering, it sounded like a coyote practicing to be a coyote.

If there was only one way to make Amy feel better, instead of a hundred, he would not have hesitated.

In a few minutes she was asleep, gripping the pillow like a flotation device, a castaway at rest at sea. The sight of her sleeping always made him a little envious, the way conversations in other languages did. He was ignored, left behind. It seemed unfair that she could close her eyes and make him, sitting right next to her, invisible. As he left the trailer, he made a lot of noise, trying unsuccessfully to wake her.

He carried the beer into the cemetery that neighbored the trailer park. The hundred-year-old tombstones were crooked, like tombstones in a Halloween play. KILLED BY INDIANS, some of them said. The ground was loamy and uneven, and he suspected he was stepping on unmarked graves, so he found a bench and, sipping the beer, watched a distant quiver of spotlights spread out and revolve and reconverge in precise increments, brusquely sweeping the sky.

When he was a child, his mother took him to an Indian mound. He was excited for days beforehand but it was just a big green lump scattered with railroad ties. The sort of place you visited without leaving your car. In protest, Tad began running up the mound and down, up and down. A man in a blue uniform stopped him and said, "You're running on the bones of my people."

The man's lips held a toothpick. He clenched his jaw, a sheriff ready to pull his gun. He smiled. "Just kidding," he said. "About my people, I mean, not the bones."

Tad thought of a few things he would've said to the man now. His thoughts were a junkyard. He hounded the edges, distracted by any oddity or shiny trinket.

The spotlights danced in the sky as he finished the beer and began constructing a list of demands for himself and Amy. It went: We must take care of each other. We must be the best versions of ourselves. We must inoculate each other from unhappiness.

Contented, feeling as if something serious had been achieved with very little effort, he walked back to the trailer. A pair of tombstones were pitched against each other in an interesting way, and Tad scrutinized them like something he might sketch. He felt expansive, blameless, a bit drunk. "Just passing through," he said to the tombstones. He said it how Gar Floyd would. He made it sound dusty.

All night a harsh wind shook the trailer on its moorings and he brought the sound into sleep with him, dreaming that they were being pulled down the highway. Into the unknown, into the unknown. In the morning he was awoken by the ticking of the trailer's metal ceiling in the sun.

They ate breakfast in a diner with framed articles on the wall about paranormal phenomena. They took a tour of the copper mine, which was cold and long and garishly informative. Amy sat with the disposable camera in her lap waiting for something photogenic to occur. Their guide, who'd worked in the mine before it closed, said everyone on the train had to ask one question before the tour ended. "Any advice for me and my new wife?" Tad asked him.

The guide thought about it for a second, then said, "Never don't say good night."

Afterward they went into antique stores and picked things up and set them down. Amy bought a piece of petrified wood that said OFFICIAL ARIZONA SOUVENIR and a dream catcher for Gar Floyd's rearview mirror. This cheered them for a while. A trifle distresses, a trifle consoles, wasn't that how it went? They looked around for consoling trifles. They returned to the trailer and listened to the radio shows.

A man keeps seeing someone who looks exactly like him. A woman begins speaking another language, one that no one, including her, understands. The shows were really about aloneness, Tad decided. He helped Amy pull off her tank top and then licked a line straight down her back. He licked dots along each side of the line, like a surgical scar. He studied her back and tried to decide what else to do.

What else was there to do?

●

The Volvo had been moved to the front of the service station, one fan blowing into the driver's-side door, another into the passenger's side. Beneath the wiper blade was a piece of paper, which Tad freed. THE HAPPY HAWKER, it said. WE PAY TOP DOLLARS FOR IMPORTS. There was a drawing of a car with dollar signs for headlights.

He leaned in. The odor, though not as harsh, was still there. Still insistent. The remains of the remains outlived the remains, Tad thought. And the wildflower bouquet remained on the dashboard. It looked happy there.

Inside the station, the old mechanic sat eating a sandwich half wrapped in wax paper. He listened to a portable radio and chewed in rhythm, as if eating the song.

"Still stinks," Tad said. "Any more fans?"

The mechanic swallowed thoughtfully before speaking. "People used to put dead fish inside hubcaps, as a joke. Maybe someone's playing a joke on you."

"I told you, it's not my car. It's Gar Floyd's."

"Maybe someone's playing a joke on Gar Floyd."

"Maybe. And maybe we're all clowns in a giant circus."

"Maybe."

The other mechanic came in from the garage and whispered something to the old man, who said, "Christ," and stood up with his sandwich. They walked outside. Tad followed them behind the station, where, in a packed-dirt clearing, Jeff was stooped over the picked carcass of what looked like a turkey. When he saw the three men, his front shoulders went rigid and he took the carcass's spine in his mouth, waiting, it appeared, for a reason to run away with it.

"He acts like we don't feed him," the younger mechanic said.

The old man breathed through his nose. "He's not acting

like anything, Lon. It's instinct. He's made to think every meal's his last. It's how he survives."

"I bet he'd bite me if I tried to snatch it from him."

"What would you do if someone tried to take away your last meal?"

Tad had the feeling that this exchange had occurred before, perhaps hundreds of times. After a while, Jeff relaxed and began gnawing at the carcass, crunching the bones ostentatiously.

"Stranded in Bisbee," the old man said finally, continuing to admire his dog and eat his sandwich. "That could be a hit song. It'd be sad, but not too sad."

"Something's wrong with this place," Tad said. It was one of those things that he didn't know he was going to say until he said it. "We were happy till we got here."

"What rhymes with Bisbee?" the old man said.

"Frisbee," the other mechanic said.

Tad waited for something else to happen. The old man bit so close to the wax paper that Tad was sure he was going to take a hunk out of it, but the old man knew, apparently he knew, what he was doing.

•

Tad and Amy had dinner in town. He ordered a buffalo burger, because he thought it might make things more exciting, but it didn't. The way the waitress handed him the plate and said, "Here's your buffalo," and then later,

"How's your buffalo?" and then, "How *was* your buffalo?" depressed him. He felt like a baby with a toy. A man at a nearby table said to the young boy across from him, "Pretty soon you'll get to sleep in a bulldozer. How's that sound?"

The boy seemed suspicious but interested.

Amy smiled from time to time to let Tad know their mutual silence was okay. The smile was a token that stood for something to say. It reminded him of the edge of a curtain being lifted and let go.

A group of waiters came out of the kitchen singing "Happy Birthday." One of them presented a single-candled cupcake to the boy, set a coffee filter atop his head, and told him to make a wish. The boy kept his eyes shut a very long time, then, all of a sudden, his face came alive again and he blew out the candle.

Tad said, "I keep thinking of that stupid commercial that goes, 'If this hammerhead stops moving, he dies.'" He tossed a napkin over his half-eaten burger. "It's probably not even true."

Amy looked at him solemnly and said, "There is so much we don't know about the hammerhead."

They laughed and then it was quiet again.

"For my birthday one year," she said, "my dad gave me *The Odyssey*, the children's version. There's a part where Odysseus returns home disguised as a shepherd to claim his wife. His dog is old and blind, but he sniffs him and immediately recognizes him. I loved that part. That's what I always thought my husband would be like."

"Like Odysseus," Tad said.

"No," Amy said. "Like his dog."

They waited for the check. Tad took Amy's hand and kissed it, inhaling the brackish sea smell of zinc oxide. She brushed crumbs off his T-shirt. He had a premonition of her doing the same thing fifty years from now, so familiar to each other they'd be strangers. He thought: there is so much and so little we don't know about each other.

•

Back in the trailer, he was restless. More sex? They'd already had sex twice. Doing it again would be strictly remedial; it would diagnose their dissatisfaction. Instead he complained about the trailer, which was starting to seem like a decoration left out too long. The carpet was filthy. The trash can was filled with condom wrappers and used condoms. Tad threw away an uneaten orange to make the trash can look more domestic.

Then he had an idea. In his wallet was a Drive Way business card with the phone number of Gar Floyd's motel in Jacksonville. He found the card and dialed the number. After the clerk connected him to Gar Floyd's room, it rang five times before someone on the other end picked up, fumbled the receiver, and said hello.

Amy studied his expression. "Who is it?" she whispered.

"Gar Floyd?" Tad asked. Gar Floyd said *yes* tentatively, as if expecting bad news. He sounded nothing like Gar Floyd.

"You don't know me," Tad said, "but I'm driving your car to Florida. I wanted to tell you that I, that we've, been wondering about you. You spend time in a person's car and you begin to wonder about him."

"Abort," Amy said, waving her hands. "Abort."

Tad had forgotten why he originally wanted to call. Gar Floyd was clearing his throat, breathing roughly. What had he expected Gar Floyd to say? "Oh," he said. "I thought you were calling from the hospital. My wife's getting treatment. She's sick."

"I'm sorry to hear that," Tad said.

"They prescribed these sleeping pills and, ever since, I keep dreaming I'm back in the Air Force. I'm doing something wrong but no one will tell me what. That's just what it was like." He paused to catch his breath. "Listen, my wife's not doing so well. What time is it where you are?"

Tad looked at his watch and told him.

"Well," Gar Floyd said after a while, "how's the car?"

"It's great," Tad said. "It's a great car."

"The transmission's been rebuilt. The tires are brand-new."

"The tires," Tad said, "are unbelievable." He felt his stomach tighten. "We shouldn't have bothered you."

"Who's there with you?"

"Amy, my wife. We're just married." Telling him this, Tad remembered that this was what he'd called to tell him. He thought it would be funny to tell Gar Floyd about getting married. "We're in Arizona."

Amy stared straight ahead, implacable, like a rigidly disciplined athlete.

"What a great time," Gar Floyd was saying. "Careless."

"Sure," Tad said. "We're seeing all there is to see. Your car's in good hands, that's what I called to tell you. We're checking all the fluids, using high octane. You'll have it in a few days."

"I've got a rental now," Gar Floyd said. "An Escort. It's a lousy car. The wind blows it all over the road. What kind of car do you drive?"

Tad drove an Escort. He didn't say anything. He watched Amy flop down on the bed and thought about his lousy, beef-brown Escort and waited for Gar Floyd to ask another question.

"You woke me up," Gar Floyd said. "The least you can do is talk to me."

Silence on both ends of the line, Tad in Arizona and Gar Floyd in Florida. Tad apologized again. He wished Gar Floyd and his wife well. He stressed the imminence of their arrival. Good-bye, he said. All right, Gar Floyd said.

He sat next to Amy on the bed and patted her arm while she studied the ceiling. "Just married," she said. "Just married. Say it one way and it sounds like one thing. Say it another way and it sounds like something else."

"I thought it'd be funny. It wasn't. What do you want me to say?"

"Nothing, everything. I want you to know when to be serious. Act like this means something."

"I'm excited we're married, I'm ecstatic."

"I'm not just talking about being married."

"What then?"

"This. This moment we're in. Life, Jesus, look at me, you never look at me."

Indeed, Tad was staring at the percolator on the counter, at its clear nipple, using it as a focal point. He looked at Amy, at her wide, wary face. Whenever she exerted herself, her cheeks flushed with ghost acne, like fingerprints on a steamed-up mirror.

She put her hand under his chin and held it strangely. She didn't blink for a long time. "What are you doing?" he asked her.

She let go and said, "Wishing."

After Tad turned off the lamp, passing headlights lurched and danced inside the trailer. He watched them for a few minutes and resolved to leave town in the morning, whether the odor was gone or not. El Paso, Houston, Baton Rouge. He wanted to be looking at Bisbee through a telescope of better days.

"Good night," he said.

"Good night," she said.

In the morning they walked their luggage to the service station. The Volvo was no longer in front, nor was it inside the garage. Looking around, Tad was surprised by the relief he felt, the sense of absolution.

"Where'd it go?" Amy asked.

Mexico, he hoped, where it'd be stripped, sold, scattered.

"They probably just moved it," he said.

Inside the office, the two mechanics sat next to each other, reading sections of the same newspaper. The younger mechanic looked up and grinned at Tad while the old man kept reading. Jeff was sleeping on a folded towel in the corner, beneath a sign for Bar's Leaks.

"My partner thinks he had an epiphany," the old man said.

"It came to me in a dream," the other man said.

Tad looked at Amy, who had her arms folded over her chest. She knew he was looking at her, he could tell by how her expression went vacant. The four walked behind the station, Jeff trailing them. The Volvo sat in the clearing with its doors open.

The younger attendant ran to the car, gawkily animated. He arched forward and leaned in for a big, cartoon sniff. "Delightful," he said.

"Potpourri," the old man said, shaking his head. "Lime-scented."

"Country summer lime," the other mechanic said. "Get in! It smells so damn clean in here!"

Tad and Amy sat in the backseat, their feet crunching down on something as they got in. Tad saw that the floorboards were filled with dark green wood shavings and dried buds. Inhaling the sweet-sour smell, he was reminded of those scented soaps he was always tempted to take a bite out of. The dead-snake odor was no longer perceptible.

"It isn't bad," Tad said. "It's better than it was."

"My girlfriend buys it in bulk. This is what my bathroom smells like."

The old man sat down in the passenger's seat. Tad hadn't noticed how big he was until he got into the car. He had to slouch forward so his head didn't touch the ceiling. Jeff jumped onto his lap and laid his snout on the headrest, panting.

"No charge," the other mechanic said. "That's the best part."

Tad reached down and grabbed a handful of the rough, ridged wood and then let it go. "No charge," he said to Amy.

"On the road again," she said, holding her hand out for Jeff to sniff, which he did, and then looked around warily. "Will you hand me that?" she said, pointing to the bouquet on the dashboard. The old man groaned as he reached forward and then handed it back to her. It looked brittle, careworn. She held it in her lap.

"No charge!" the young mechanic said. He started the car and pulled out of the clearing, kicking up loose dirt.

Out front, Tad loaded the car. He hung the dream catcher on the rearview mirror while Amy drove off, waving to the mechanics, who responded with succinct nods. As they headed east into New Mexico, the landscape started to make sense again and Tad felt an agreeable recession. Time, he knew, was vast—seen from a distance, each moment was nothing, a ripple, barely perceptible, nothing. Soon they would stop at a rest area and make love while other travelers gamboled in their designated areas. They'd stay in a motel shaped like a teepee. By the time they arrived in Florida with Gar Floyd's car, Bisbee would be no more than a minor lay-over, a place where—look, here's a picture, Amy and Tad smiling at the shrine—they were as happy as they'd ever be.

border to border

Maxim lost his crown. He was eating in Small
World's employee cafeteria, already feeling thrown
off by big, pink-necked Miss Beebee, who existed,
as far as Maxim could tell, solely to throw him off.
At the buffet line, she dumped a spatula-ful of Irish
lasagna into his bowl, tapped the spatula twice on
the side, and said, "You're beautiful, too." She read

his name tag. "It's a beautiful world, Maxim from Estonia, filled with beautiful people."

"More sauce, please," he said.

"Me and you, we got the kind of beauty that don't expire." She dumped grayish sauce into his bowl. "*Interior* beauty. *Bone* beauty. *Psychological* beauty. Know what I mean?"

"No," he told her. "My English, it's not nearly that good yet."

At a table next to some Chinese acrobats in silk costumes, he ate Miss Beebee's latest attempt to gastronomically unite two cultures: cabbage and noodles and red sauce and fatty shreds of mutton—

He bit down on something hard, like a pebble. He tried to work it to the front of his mouth to spit it into a napkin— when into the cafeteria walked Paula. Tall, lovely, impervious American Paula. Paula with hair so soft-looking Maxim wanted to snip some to wear as a mustache. She worked in the Global Superpowers Pavilion with the other cheerful propagandists. Her job was to ask people filing out of the *Operation: Emancipation!* musical, "Do you have any questions about freedom?"

She moved through the cafeteria with the rehearsed poise of a gymnast on a beam, greeting everyone. Maxim held his breath, along with the food, the pebble, whatever it was, in his mouth. He waited.

"*Arigato,*" she said to the table of Chinese acrobats.

"*Hola,*" to a Central American couple. To Maxim: "And how are *you?*"

He swallowed the mouthful of food. He nodded. He smiled. He was, he told her, wonderful.

While Paula ordered, he inadvertently ran his tongue over his rearmost lower molar. In place of the crown that had sat there for the past ten years, there was a jagged crag of tooth. He could taste dental glue and decay, a bleating, blood-warm tang. Stealing a last glance at Paula at the gyro bar, he cleared his tray.

One look at Paula and nobody, Maxim was certain, could have any questions about freedom.

•

Health Services was on the northern hemisphere of Small World, which was laid out like a world map, with different-colored border lines separating each of the countries. Maxim walked to the dentist's through an onrush of visitors. Men in sunglasses and visors and women with noisy, cheerless breasts. Foreign tourists hustling to miniaturized versions of their native lands. What did they find? If they were lucky and from Germany, they found a beer garden, a 3-D movie about knife-making, and the Putsch, a steel roller coaster. If they were from Estonia, they found Maxim and his fake Estonian coworker, Danni, in a modified gypsy cart beneath a leprous oak, selling an array of bells.

Maxim was traversing Scotland when a couple stopped

him. The woman studied his uniform—lavender peasant hat, peasant shirt, peasant pants. She covered his name tag with her hand and said, "Venezuela?"

Maxim pointed west.

She gripped the name tag and said, "Wait now. Nepal."

He pointed east.

"He obviously doesn't know English," the man said. "I mean, look at him. He has one of those faces like, 'I have suffered some unspeakable shit.'"

"He has to know where he's *from* in English." Turning to Maxim: "Okay: Malaysia, Serbia, Hungary, Turkey, Nicaragua, Argentina, China, Peru."

Maxim nodded and the woman said, "Peru? Peru! He's from Peru!" and Maxim continued nodding until she released his name tag.

"Hooray," the man said sarcastically.

•

In the dentist's chair, Maxim studied smeared fingerprints on the adjustable light. They seemed to imply a struggle. The dentist rolled in on a low stool. "Broke your crown," he said. "And Jill came tumbling after?"

When Maxim didn't reply, the dentist said, "Old joke." He snapped on a pair of blue latex gloves. "Allergic to these?"

"I don't know," Maxim said. "I've never eaten one."

"Hot damn," the dentist said. Attached to his glasses was a device like a jeweler's loupe, and when the dentist leaned over, Maxim saw himself mirrored in convex glass, his face fixed like a happy cadaver.

While the dentist browsed Maxim's mouth, Maxim thought about his tooth. Originally, he'd broken it on a frosted cookie in his parents' doughnut shop in Delray Beach, where they emigrated when he was ten. His mother had been examining a dollar bill on which I OWNED SLAVES had been stamped over George Washington's tired head. She made tut-tutting sounds—not about the owning of slaves, but the defiling of dollar bills—when Maxim bit into the cookie. He'd tried to hide it then, too. Covering his mouth with his hand, he watched his mother dump out four quarters from the cystic fibrosis jar and replace them with the sullied dollar.

"Not bad," the dentist said. "Not a bit bad. Some Eastern Euros open their mouths and . . ." He shook his head solemnly. "Dresden. Crushed bridgework, missing teeth, gum disease, canines ground to the root. The teeth tell me everything. You've had an easy life. You favor the right side when you chew. The dentist who did that crown went to a state school in the Midwest."

Maxim's chair pitched forward. "Are we done?" he asked.

The dentist snapped off the gloves and made notes on the chart. "All we can do is wait for that crown. Shouldn't be more than a day, give or take, right?"

Maxim rinsed and spit, rinsed and spit. "Will it be expensive?"

"How do you mean?"

"The new crown. I don't have dentist insurance."

The dentist nodded, agreeing not with Maxim but in recognition of the oversight. "How to put this." He bit his lip. "The crown you swallowed, it's fine. It broke off clean. You just need to . . . fish . . . no, *retrieve* it the next time you—"

"Wait, wait. Please," Maxim interrupted. "You're not asking me to search my feces for a fake tooth, which you can then put back in my mouth, are you? So that every time I eat I can be reminded of my feces?"

"Maxim, if you want a pretty new crown, we can do that. It'll be about sixteen hundred dollars, but we can do it. You also have cavities that need filling."

Maxim ran his tongue over the tooth, remembering how his mom had insisted he tell the first dentist to just pull the tooth. No one will ever see it, she said. You have plenty more teeth. Maxim never told him this. He lied and told her the man refused to pull it.

"I'm here for you regardless," the dentist said, forming the latex gloves into a ball. He rolled into the hall to wash his hands. And then, with a little too much glee: "You're the one who has to look at himself in the mirror."

•

Back in his dormitory, an hour before work, Maxim looked at himself in the mirror. He found that if he squinted while flexing the muscles along his jawline, he could make himself into a somewhat interesting-looking tragedy victim.

The kind of a man women thought about only in retrospect, after seeing his picture in the paper next to a story about a bungled carjacking or accidental carbon monoxide poisoning.

I remember *him*, they would say. Maxim had done some thinking about this. They'd recall him as the man they didn't spend enough time admiring. We mistook his shyness for gloom! they would say. We failed to see how secretly handsome he was. And now he was gone, poor, overlooked Maxim.

Their hypothetical pity comforted him.

At this moment, the crown wended its way through his upper digestive tract, confused, still pretending to be a tooth. Maxim felt sorry for the crown. He felt sorry for Maxim. Sixteen hundred dollars was about two hundred and fifty hours in the bell cart. He couldn't call his mother, his mother had no money either.

He fell asleep to the sound of televisions in adjoining dorms, and woke up feeling crushed beneath some ogre's calloused thumb. Still unsure whether or not he would retrieve the tooth. Mostly he didn't want to think about it. Some decisions you dwelled on for days, carefully clarifying them like calculus problems, enjoying the steady tumble toward a verdict. This was not one of those decisions.

•

Maxim and Danni watched teenagers run by the cart on their way to Germany's roller coaster. "Come here!" Danni yelled. When one complied, he said, "First off, slow the fuck down. Second off, come look at these amazing hand-crafted bells."

Danni's real name was Danny. He was Dominican, but he didn't get along with his countrymen in the Caribbean section, so he'd been reassigned a month ago. He possessed a pinpoint malevolence, which was invigorating until he focused it on you. He was also an enthusiastic salesman, fearless, volatile, ineffective.

Later, when the line to the Putsch stretched past the bell cart, a man with hostile blond hair knocked on the counter and said, "Tell me three things about Estonia."

Danni turned to Maxim, and Maxim said what he always said: "We're on the Baltic below Finland. Our most recent revolution consisted of a human chain. Millions of citizens organized a peaceful protest by holding hands from border to border and singing for our freedom. Millions of us. It was stunning. I was young but I participated."

The line to the Putsch inched forward and the man did, too. He thanked Maxim for the information, no doubt simultaneously voiding it from memory.

"We also make bells," Danni added, pulling a large bell from its hook. "All day long, bells bells bells. It's all we do!"

The man couldn't hear him. Danni was holding the feature model, a brass-plated bell manufactured in Vietnam, which sold for $11.50.

"We don't really make bells in Estonia," Maxim told Danni after the line thinned out.

Danni scrutinized the bell for a long time. "Then how come me and you are out here sweating in this dogsled of bells? Over in the Dominican, my people are selling six different kinds of iced drinks. Christ. What do we make in Estonia?"

"Toilet tissue. Car parts, I think. Lumber."

"Goddamn." Danni returned the bell to the hook, silencing the chime with his thumb. "It's a good thing we left that shithole."

Maxim walked to Russia to use their water fountain. When he returned, a teenage girl was sitting on a stool in front of the Bell Cart, listening while Danni spoke with his eyes closed. The girl, fleshily pretty, was swinging her bare feet.

"All of us holding hands," Danni said, "like this." He reached for the girl's hand. "Border to border, singing for freedom and glory and shit. It was just . . . I can't even explain in English. You know the feeling you get in your heart when you're making love to several people at a time?"

Apparently the girl, who let go of Danni's hand and walked off, didn't know the feeling. Maxim sat on her stool. The wood was warm from her thighs. "I asked you not to tell that story. That's my story."

"Your story?" Danni kicked the bottom of the cash register. "You think anyone cares about your dusty-ass country?" He looked at all the bells, plainly angered by them. "*Estonia. It sounds like a damn larva or a venereal disease.*"

"Estonia's not dusty, Danni. If anything it's muddy."

"Dusty, muddy. It don't matter. I just make stuff up when you're gone, Maxim. I tell people our highest elevation's a trash pile. That our chief exports are clowns and rape. That our government's run by some goats and dogs and pregnant cats and—"

"*Enough!*" Maxim shouted. He was gratified by the little jolt it caused Danni, the flashbulb-stunned silence. "People's homes aren't for you to joke about. You should try thinking a few things you don't say."

Danni gathered himself and leaned into the counter separating them. "And you," he said, "should try some mouthwash. Because your breath smells dead like that hot-sausage water in Germany's Dumpster."

Danni laughed, hopped off his stool, walked away. Maxim switched seats and pushed PLAY on the folk music CD that management had provided, a jangle of strings and bleating and moaning, like the soundtrack to a murder. He began to feel pulled backward. He thought of the human chain stretching from the northern border to the southern border of his country. His mother to his left, his father to his right, Maxim was connected to the lakes and to the sea. The chain ran past their house, white clapboard with blackbirds loitering on the eaves and a feeble reef of smoke above the chimney. He imagined they sang songs like the one currently playing, but he couldn't remember ever hearing anyone sing while he lived there. Not even the birds. Before the chain dispersed, his mother had leaned down, let go of his hand to wipe his face, and said, with her customary look of grim inspection, "We will never be happier."

He'd returned to Tallinn once, with a former girlfriend, Lori. They went to attend the funeral of Maxim's great-aunt. Whenever one of Maxim's relatives chatted at her in Estonian, she nodded and smiled. "I'm just here," she answered very slowly, "to show my support."

The way she showed her support was by telling everyone she was showing her support. Maxim's cousin, who spoke some English, took him aside and asked, "Who is this woman? What is her sport?"

Tallinn was flower stalls and tubercular houses and rebar skeletons holding together heaps of rubble and him and Lori arguing constantly: on the open-air bus through his old neighborhood, which had been razed and replaced with tract housing. They argued in the city park where he used to play soccer, now overtaken by panhandlers and fake veterans. They argued in bed before going to sleep and just after waking up. Maxim wasn't good at arguing. He didn't have the stamina. After a while they'd argue about the way they were arguing, Lori's nostrils flaring like hog nostrils, and Maxim would feel like jabbing his thumb into her eye or biting her tricep, something resolute and silencing, something unforgivable.

They held hands as they walked through Old Town, each daring the other to let go first. She stood on the stairs of St. Olav's and Maxim took her picture, clipping off her head at the scalp. A pitiful gesture, but momentarily gratifying. He kissed her afterward, tasting her makeup.

He missed Lori. A few hours with her, or a tolerable likeness, would cure just about everything. Lori was not beautiful, but she was kind and she had fat memorable thighs. She was studying to be a neonatal nurse; she wanted to work with preemies. Right now Maxim would like to rest his head in Lori's lap and pretend he was a preemie. Too tiny for the world, he needed to steal Lori's warmth. How generous she was. How easy his life was. As lucid and hummable as a song about life . . .

"Bells," he called. "The singing fruits of my homeland."

A grubby feeling scraped along his abdomen.

What he needed was the kind of nurse who examined your injuries and declared them superficial.

He breathed. He tried to rid himself of himself.

An elderly woman approached the cart and asked, "Am I in Turkey, sweetheart?"

"You're in Estonia," Maxim said, shielding his mouth with his hand. "Land of bells and mud and toilet tissue. Welcome."

The woman's face grew delighted and sincere, the face of

a child selecting a teddy bear. "You are so cute in that little costume. I could eat you up."

"I assure you," Maxim said, "I would not taste good at all. You should eat someone from a Mediterranean country. A Sicilian perhaps."

"Now you see, that's a language barrier. *Eat you up*'s a saying. It just means I like you."

"Ah, interesting. Tell me something," Maxim said. "Would you ever search through your own feces for a tooth if you had no money to buy a new one?"

The woman backed away very slowly, her upper body remaining stiff while her legs took her away. Maxim waved good-bye. "Bells," he called to the park-goers streaming by. "Bells. Made by hand, with love, for you."

•

The alimentary canal might sound like an enchanted place where lovers share a paddleboat and whisper lies to each other, but it is actually the tubular passage between the mouth and the anus. Three days later, Maxim's crown sat in the lower portion of his alimentary canal—the jejunum of his small intestine, to be exact—while Maxim sat in the employee cafeteria, studying Miss Beebee's vilest invention yet, cheeseburger sushi.

"This is no food," he said to her when she handed it to him. "This is a crime against food. What about some cereal? Maybe a simple banana."

"You need to realize," Miss Beebee said, "I'm not cooking just for you, Maxim from Estonia. Do you know there are cultures who'd rather eat a bowl of tadpoles than a bowl of cereal? Cultures that regard bananas like we would a filled baby diaper? I'm cooking for every single country in the world. This involves compromise. You know what compromise means? It means not getting what you want. You know what not getting what you want means?"

"Yes, Miss Beebee, I know exactly what it means."

"I always say if you can't eat the thing you love, love the thing you eat."

"Talking to you always makes me so sad."

Maxim wasn't hungry anyhow. He sat at a table and sipped his water, aware of the other diners staring at him. Somehow, news of the broken crown, and of his attendant difficulty, had spread through the park. The dentist had called a few days ago, his voice sounding brittle and strange. "Everyone here's behind you," he said. Maxim heard music and loud voices in the background. "And there's unanimous agreement on the dire nature of your situation."

At the next table, a man in white linen offered a tentative thumbs-up. He waited for Maxim to return it.

Maxim frowned.

"Fig juice," the man shouted. "It make bowels into factory!"

As Maxim was about to clear his tray, Paula walked into the cafeteria. She wore the same uniform, but something was awry. Her hair? No, her hair was still immaculate, softened by gilded tongues. She said hello to everyone, deftly fitting one greeting to the next without a seam. She approached Maxim's table and he quickly wiped his hand over his mouth and steeled himself. The phrase *filled baby diaper* had taken residence in his mind and would not leave. Was she wearing new lip gloss? Her lips were certainly glossy, but it appeared so natural, an innate gloss . . .

She sat down across from him. She gathered his hands into hers. Her hands felt—he was too overwhelmed to discern single impressions. It was like trying to evaluate the craftsmanship of a knife that was stabbing you. "We've been talking about you all day," she said.

"I am." Maxim cleared his throat several times. "Happy."

He listened to Paula as closely as he could. She was saying all kinds of significant things. "Freedom's being able to choose," she said. "Having choices, being free. That's why it's called freedom, Maxim."

The moment she said his name, he ceased to pay attention. *Maxim.* It fell from her mouth like a spit-smoothed pearl. He studied her lips while they lifted, contorted, connected, made words, a necklace of words. She seemed to be discussing his recent trip to the dentist. So she, too, had heard. Maxim registered this and stashed his embarrassment in a faraway pouch. She was saying, "No one should have to touch his own poo. No one with a choice. No one with freedom, Maxim."

Again! His name was, like, *cascading* out of her mouth. She scrubbed it of casualness and habit, suffused it with magic. Maxim. He must've been a king in a past life. Or at least one who worked very closely with a king. Paula still held his hands in hers and he could, now that he was aware of it, feel delicate rivets beyond her skin. The imminence of her skeleton.

She said, "Don't do it."

"Okay."

"I mean it, Maxim. We can talk to the dentist, work out a payment plan. We have a ton of ideas to help you through this."

"This is an excellent coincidence." Maxim felt himself lose contact with coherency. "Yes, I would like some help from your ton of ideas."

Paula gripped his hand one last time before letting go. "The coincidence is that I'm totally into coincidences. And helping people."

"I enjoy to be helped. It is my favorite thing."

"Another coincidence," Paula said.

After she left, Miss Beebee approached his table and said, "Maxim from Estonia, you need to close your mouth when a pretty girl talks to you. Girls don't want to be stared at like optical illusions. You didn't see me waving? I was like, *Close your mouth*. You got to act like you been there before."

Maxim studied his cheeseburger sushi, congealing on his

plate into something moist and unmentionable; he studied Miss Beebee, pink-necked and avid but softened by concern. She looked like a character on a package of sweets. He said, "What if I've never been there?"

Miss Beebee laughed. "Start pretending."

•

If not for the events of the past few days, Maxim would have recognized this as sound advice. Combined with his glee at hearing Paula say *Maxim*, it might have reminded him of when he brought his marching-band vest to the shop in Delray Beach to have his name embroidered on the pocket. Maybe the counterwoman was hard of hearing, because when he picked it up a week later, stitched in gold cursive on the pocket was ROBBY. He paid her and dutifully wore the vest during football games while he banged cymbals and counted steps. His bandmates began calling him Robby, then friends of his bandmates, then friends of the friends. "Robby's here!" they'd say. "Robby's running things!"

He wore the vest to school. He liked being Robby. Robby was loosely hinged, hazardous to women. Maxim napped with his hands in his underwear and was still afraid to watch *The Wizard of Oz*, but Robby wasn't afraid of any goddamn thing. Robby laughed at flying monkeys. Robby studied the crowd during halftime, confident they were there just to watch him bang his cymbals. He didn't need to explain where he came from. He didn't need to create digestible capsule versions of his country. Robby was like *night*. You didn't hear people asking night where it came from, did you?

One day some kids from marching band came into the doughnut shop. When they left, each said good-bye to Robby, and Maxim spent two hours explaining to his mom who Robby was.

"Maxim is your name. It means *greatest*," she said. "What does Robby mean?"

"Danger, I think. Or a kind of leather."

"You are not a kind of leather," she said in Estonian. "You are Maxim."

Yes, he was Maxim. Short, unlovely, pervious Maxim. Maxim with the hairy neck and donkey laugh. Maxim with the telltale clothes. The irregular-fit pants, the imitation American T-shirt that said WARNING: HOT SUMMER PROP-ERTY. Maxim who was too busy learning English and selling doughnuts to acquire a hobby.

Maxim who since arriving in the United States had grown very good at pretending. Later in the day, in fact, sitting in the bell cart with Danni, he pretended to be uninterested in a story of how he, Danni, had seduced one of the Angolan candle dancers the night before.

"To hell with big countries," Danni was saying. "Brazil, China. Go right for one you never heard of. This woman, her name is . . . I forget. She's black, you realize. I tell her all the lies people've been spreading about Angola, and make it up as I go. I put my arm around her and say, 'I've always been a fierce supporter of your people. Tonight we're gonna show everyone that love has no borders.' Thirty minutes later we're in her shower, naked, and you can guess the rest." He paused. "Nah, I'll tell you, so you don't guess wrong."

Maxim stared over the trees at a sky the color of fogged-up glass while Danni told him all the details of his humanitarian shower rut with the candle dancer. Though Maxim didn't run his tongue over the broken tooth, he was always aware of it. When he breathed, when his stomach hurt. "Bells," he called out feebly. He hadn't moved his bowels in five days.

"So are you or aren't you?" Danni said after a while.

"Aren't I what?"

"Gonna get that tooth?"

"I don't know. What would you do?"

Danni shook his head. "I'd've made myself cack the second I swallowed it. But now . . . hell, it wouldn't even be a question with me. Course I'd do it. What's the big deal? Someone might find out? Have you ever studied prison behavior, Maxim?"

"No," Maxim said.

"I have. And you'd be surprised what you can talk yourself into if you don't have a choice either way. It's how your brain lets you live with yourself. Otherwise, there's some people who'd just wake up every morning screaming and crying. People in prison, for instance, those fat-ass world-record twins on their motorbikes, quadriplegics, Nazis, you."

Maxim sighed. "Have you even been to prison?" he asked.

"Not yet," Danni said.

Of course it was no use talking to Danni. Still, watching the park-goers streaming by, Maxim involuntarily tried to coax himself into a decision. Since the conversation with Paula, his uncertainty had turned into fear over what she would think. She would be aloofly disappointed if he decided to keep the crown—and that would make Maxim want to jump out of a high window. It'd be easy enough to fish out (no, the doctor amended, *retrieve*) the crown, bring it to the dentist, and lie to Paula about it. But what if she found out later? Sometimes he talked in his sleep. What if one night he started talking in his sleep about the tooth and she, lying next to him, heard?

He knew he had no choice but to fish out/retrieve the crown. He just had to find a way to live with himself afterward. This was the thing, this was always the thing.

"The quicker you do it, the quicker you can start finding ways to forget it," Danni was saying. He balled up his apron and tucked it under the counter and saluted Maxim.

About an hour after Danni left, Maxim followed a sunlit silhouette as it approached the bell cart. Blond hair, stars-and-stripes uniform. He stared, unself-conscious, because clearly her presence made everything else, including him, invisible. Her smile was unhidden and benign; her gait measured to the fraction.

"Well, hello," Paula said. "So this is what Estonia looks like."

Maxim wasn't able to say anything for a long, for an irresponsibly long time. He could hear the heavy metallic ticking of the Putsch ascending its lift hill, then screams.

"We would've cleaned up if we knew you were coming," he said finally.

"It's cute." She tilted her head from side to side, roughly in time with the CD that was playing. "I love music," she said, sitting down on the wooden stool.

"This is folk music from Estonia."

"That's too funny," she said.

Maxim waited for her to explain, but apparently she felt she didn't need to. Probably it was too obvious for her to point out. Maxim laughed to show that he understood.

"We've been thinking a lot about you and your problem, Maxim," she said. She pulled a piece of paper from her breast pocket. She unfolded it to reveal a typed list of months with numbers next to each. "Here's your payment plan. Just a little each month adds up to a lot. The dentist, he's been super-nice. He agreed to not charge interest, so what you have's a really special deal."

He touched the piece of paper: it was warm. He felt a surge in his abdomen, a sensation of either love or lust or hopefulness or the idiot churning of his digestive system. "Paula," he said.

"Yes."

"Paula."

"Yes, Maxim."

"Paula. I know you're trying to help me learn about freedom. I know you have good intentions."

"Don't worry about a thing, Maxim."

"No. No, I won't worry," he said. How to phrase it? He had a tendency when he was nervous to retreat to the bluntest possibilities. It was a way of getting it over with quickly. He breathed, he waited for the right words to come. He said, "If you'd just be with me for a little while, I could force myself to get the old crown. I don't need the new crown. The old one's fine."

The right side of Paula's face twitched almost imperceptibly. "Be with you how so?"

"The usual way. Or however you want. Or I don't know."

Paula breathed deeply. "Oh. Wow. Well, gosh. Okay. Let's see. Right. That's the thing about freedom, Maxim. It can be somewhat . . . sad. Like how you just exercised your freedom to ask me to be with you? Now I have to exercise mine to say no way, but thanks. Really."

She rebuffed him congenially, brought him to the surface in stages like a scuba diver. She continued saying his name, but with less and less resonance. He started to notice things like that her gums, when she smiled, densely glistened like boiled ham. Also her face was too skinny. And her eyes were so blue they brought to mind toilet cleaner. Her tongue, where was her tongue? Oh, there it was. Yes, her tongue was actually still quite nice. He traced his own tongue along the inside of his mouth, reenacting hers, stopping on the hewn molar.

"I know what I have to do," he said. He thanked her. He even touched his hand to her hair, which was, as he had suspected, supernaturally soft. "It's a perfectly good crown."

These were the words with the strongest aftertaste. If they weren't heroic, they were at least—no, they were definitely heroic. He savored them after Paula left. He let himself savor the thought, however delusional, of her savoring them.

This was how Paula said good-bye: *Bye now.*

•

Maxim knew what he had to do, and he did it the following day. He borrowed a pair of yellow latex gloves and a sauerkraut bucket from Poland, which he toted through the park, trailed by catcalls and whistles from his fellow employees: "It's time! It's time!" In his room, he ate the recommended dose of a chocolate laxative bar, then sat on the bucket. It was as uncomfortable as he expected it would be. He tried not to envision how he would get the crown but was unable to restrain himself. In the past, when he swallowed something, it was gone, but now he involuntarily retraced the crown's journey, all the way to a permanent anchorage in his mouth. This, he considered, was why we voided solid waste from behind, so we didn't have to consider it afterward. So we could *leave* it behind.

Our bodies were explicable. They made sense when you considered them. How our faces made crude maps of what we were thinking. How our internal lives kept pushing their way to the surface.

Maxim stared at his wall, blank except for a horror movie poster left by the previous tenant. He could hear his neighbors' televisions: Spanish, Chinese, Russian, Portuguese, English. Together the televisions made a sound like the brown smear of overmixed paints. He closed his eyes and concentrated on pulling out a single language. But they were all mixed up, indecipherable.

What did he need with freedom? Having a choice only meant he was going to make the wrong choice. Like on his first birthday, when his mother held out a string, a ruble note, and a crumpled napkin, and he was supposed to select one, which would portend his future. He selected the napkin. "Ah," he now imagined his mother saying. "This means you are going to sell bells for a living. And that you'll be a nuisance to the women you want. Oh, and also one day you'll find yourself on a sauerkraut bucket, waiting for a laxative to take effect so you can extract a crown from your own feces. Happy birthday, baby Maxim."

Freedom was for the Paulas of the world. Lithe acrobats on invisible trapezes tumbling above a safety net. Maxims were better equipped for choke chains and limitation, following orders. Stand here, stay still, be thankful. Rarely had Maxim felt so liberated as when he told Paula that it was a perfectly good crown. And it was. The dentist prob-ably had all sorts of exceptional disinfectants to clean it, sterilize it, return it to new—better than new. Maybe the disinfectants came in a choice of flavors, like mouthwash. He would choose . . . no, he'd let the dentist choose.

He felt a surge in his lower torso. All the hope and toil, all the choices made and unmade had led him here, to this state of perfect choicelessness.

In the center of his room was a slatted drain, and gazing into it he could feel gravity trying to pull him toward the drain, down, down through the pipe to the center of the earth. Trying to swallow and absorb him for nutrients. First his skin then his tissue then his bones. "Meat," he sang in time with the clamor of televisions. "Meat meat meat meat meat."

He burrowed his hands into the yellow gloves. He sang another verse.

lugo in normal time

Lugo unbidden, Lugo at home in a new pair of sweatpants, holding, circling, waiting for something to happen. Something often happens.

. This weekend he has his daughter. He's sipping brandy and following her from room to room while she works on a project for school. A teacher has asked her to find a household item and use it to tell a story, so all morning Erica's been picking things up, studying them carefully, and putting them down. She roots through the boxes in his closet, boxes in the hall-way and in the kitchen. She finds a fondue set: a pot with six blue-handled and six red-handled prongs, like equipment for opposing teams. She taps one against the sink. "How about these," she says.

Lugo regards the derelict prong from the kitchen table. "Never used," he says. The idea, the hopeful logistics of him and Irene making fondue together seem ridiculous now. He remembers the old lady who sold it to them repeating, *It's so lovely, it's so lovely.* "We bought it at a yard sale before you were born," he tells Erica. "It's supposed to melt cheese."

"And you still have it why?"

"I guess it reminds me of your mother," he says.

Erica is fourteen years old. She has brought a to-do list with her, which she keeps taped to Lugo's refrigerator. This weekend, she must finish two pages of geometry problems, start *Member of the Wedding*, figure out feudalism, and go to a friend's birthday party. Lugo notices *Stay with Dad* written on the list, among her obligations.

Uneasy, he says, studying the list.

Not easy is what he means to say. His daughter's not-easiness makes him uneasy.

Earlier that day, when she dropped Erica off, Irene handed him a note. "Remember what we talked about," it said. "Ease up on the scotch. Distract yourself (and her). Maybe take her to a movie."

Lugo looks at the newspaper. Searching for the movie listings, he finds an article about a prison escape in Illinois. A prisoner sealed himself in a box with some packing peanuts and shipped himself to freedom. He jumped out of the mail truck and is still at large. At large, Lugo repeats, treasuring the sound of it. Sometimes an expression like this is all it takes. He closes the newspaper, forgets what he was going to do. Then he remembers: he was going to fix himself another drink.

•

Erica moves in long, loping strides, scrutinizing, disregarding. This is Lugo's house, his new house. Actually it's an apartment, an old apartment with broth smells and puppy and disinfectant smells in the carpet. The odor of a dozen forfeited security deposits. Most things are still in boxes from his move eight months ago. Extension cords, Halloween appliqués, ornaments, a box of old Louis L'Amour paperbacks whose covers Erica studies, bemused. She opens one of them. "'Death had come quickly and struck hard,'" she reads, "'leaving the burned wagons, the stripped and naked bodies, unnaturally white beneath the sun.' Wow. Are these yours?"

"They were when I was about your age," he says. "I was saving them."

"Not for me, I hope."

"No," Lugo says. "No, not for you."

No, not for her. Not since three seconds ago, four seconds, five. He takes sips from the edge of his drink. It's cold and warm and cold. It is a wading pool and he's just tranquilly wetting his ankles.

In his bedroom, under the bed, she finds shoeboxes of family photographs organized by shape. "Me as a baby. Me in front of a chicken shop," she says, dialing through them. "Me in front of another chicken shop."

Lugo bends down and picks up a crushed blue sock, underhands it into the closet.

"You were obsessed with the Popeyes sign," he reminds her. "Whenever we drove near it you'd chant *popeye popeye* until I pulled over and let you look at the sign. After a while, you'd say *okay* and I'd drive off."

"I don't remember."

She also liked street sweepers, bats, kangaroos, the sound of television static . . .

"Bring one of those photos to class with you. You could say, 'Once upon a time I was in love with the Popeyes sign.' It'd be a great story."

"You don't know the kids in my class," she says. "I mean, they'd *annihilate* me if I came in with something like that." She pushes the shoebox under the bed with her bare foot. Her toenails are painted black with a rim of tan-pink new-ness at the cuticle. He has asked her what the black polish means and she looked at him as if he had asked what danc-ing, what the leaf of a tree means. He remembers a song, "I wear Black on the outside 'cause Black is how I feel on the inside." Maybe that's what it means.

"They wouldn't actually annihilate you," he says to her.

The note Irene handed him was on the back of a recipe card for twice-baked potatoes. He flipped the card while climbing the stairs of his apartment with Erica and he studied the recipe as he'd studied the note. Irene's messages to him lately weren't as clear as they used to be. They leaked static and forced Lugo to listen too closely to hear anything.

Why write the note on a recipe card? Was she trying to impel him to make twice-baked potatoes? He could certainly try. Erica was sitting on the couch with her bag in her lap as he read through the recipe. All the measurements and ingredients made him tired. You needed fresh dill. And the potatoes had to be baked not once but twice.

"You still haven't unpacked your things yet," Erica said. "What are you waiting for?"

"I can't get used to this place. A few weeks ago I noticed a huge footprint on the bathroom ceiling. Right in the middle. *How'd it get there?* I think every time I'm on the toilet. It's horrible. I'm going to find a new place."

Erica organized her homework into discrete piles on the coffee table. "Do you remember anything about feudalism?" she asked.

He nodded slowly. He looked down at the recipe again. "You know," he said, studying the ingredients, "I'm not even sure I have potatoes."

At the kitchen table, Lugo wraps a gift for Erica's friend. The box is small and light—when he picks it up, it feels like there's nothing inside. This is the only reason he opens the box, to make sure it contains a present. It does: a peso tied through with a string, a necklace.

He wraps the box in slow time. Often, when he's undertaking a task that requires particular care, he switches to slow time. He folds the paper over the box and pulls off a perfectly sized piece of tape. He centers it on the paper, runs his finger over the top of it, making it invisible. He folds down each of the sides, cutting excess paper for maximum symmetry. In slow time, each movement lasts twice as long, but each is twice as efficient, so wrapping the present doesn't take any longer than it would in normal time.

Finished, he looks around for something else to wrap. The fondue set sits on the counter. It looks so stupid. He fixes another brandy, a nod to Irene's request to ease up on the scotch, and he feels suddenly impatient for Christmas. Stringing popcorn and cranberries and mulling wine and all the other things they should have done and never did.

They, he and Irene, treated time like it didn't mean anything, that was the main problem. They forgot how the past moves aside for the present, and the present moves aside for the future, and what that leaves you with is a ceaseless series of transitions. Ceaseless, one after the other, alignment to re-alignment. It's hard! How do people not drink? Drinking's actually the only thing to do about it. To hem all that jagged edging and make the intolerable tolerable. Now that he and Irene aren't together, he's able to navigate all the transitions he has to.

He brings the fondue set to the table, sets the prongs atop the pewter pot, and measures out wrapping paper. There isn't enough to wrap everything, so he wraps just the prongs, sets them next to the box.

Erica walks into the kitchen holding a clear plastic bag of hair. "This?"

"That," he says, "is a bag of hair."

"Whose hair?"

"Your mother's, but we pretended it was yours. So." Erica turns away, he's boring her. "It's a good story." She walks into the hall with the hair. It's actually not a good story. "Don't you want to hear the story?"

"I can't bring a bag of hair to school, Dad," she calls back. "I have to go get ready for Adrienne's."

"Why can't you bring hair to school? Didn't you just ask me what it was?"

He hears nimble feet scurrying up the carpeted stairs. The door of the spare bedroom shutting lightly.

He sips his brandy, which tastes how smoke and feet smell, agreeably disagreeable. They neglected to collect the hair after Erica's first haircut, so Irene snipped some of her own hair and put it in a bag. Why in the world were they saving hair? Did they think they were Mayans? He and Irene thought memories could be safely housed within souvenirs; that was one of the other main problems.

Irene is a potter. It took her nearly ten years to establish herself, and it happened by accident when a gallery owner asked if she'd be insulted if she, the gallery owner, marketed Irene's box-shaped pots as funeral urns. Soon people from all over the world were mailing her the cremains of their loved ones. She would fire and burnish the pot with leaf patterns, then pour in the cremains and seal it with wire and beads.

She used to let Lugo destroy the pots she wasn't happy with. He'd put on an apron, load the pots onto a dolly, push them into the backyard, and use a hammer with an antler handle to crack them. Few things before or since have been as satisfying. The terra-cotta shattered with a *plink* and Lugo would be left with shards to study before he threw them into a garbage bag. What was wrong with these pots? he wondered. They always looked fine to him. He never asked.

Lugo gargles mouthwash until he can no longer stand it. He waits in fast time for Erica to come downstairs.

•

Driving to the party, he searches for something interesting to say. Last night he dreamed he was hiding in a barn from a tornado. Today he read about a man who mailed himself to freedom. He could ask a question, but his questions are too general (How's school? Life? Your mother?) or too needling

(What are you thinking about? Why are you so quiet? Do you know you didn't used to be so quiet?). In front of them is a van with a license plate that says I BREW, which he points out to Erica. She nods without looking at it.

"I used to brew, you know," Lugo says. "Back then. When I brewed. You wouldn't remember."

"What are you talking about?"

"Just testing you. Making sure you're paying attention. You pass."

Erica opens the glove compartment and closes it. She wears a short dress with a cacophony of letters along the mid-riff. Her hair is tied into twin braids and pulled back. She looks pretty, older. Stopped at a red light, he asks, "What do you want for Christmas? I think I'll do some shopping while you're at the party."

"I haven't really thought about it."

"Well, think about it. I want to get you what you want."

"Dad, it's March. I have like a billion things to do before Christmas." She opens the glove compartment again, closes it. "Light's green."

He drives slowly, stalling for time. He turns on the radio, cycles through the preprogrammed stations. All the songs are love songs. He turns it off.

"I'm gonna go through my things when I get home," he says. "I'll find something for your class."

"There's stuff at Mom's I can use. It's no big deal. I was just teasing you about the hair. Don't worry."

He laughs. He feels strange, as if caught in that brief gap between glimpsing himself in a mirror and recognizing the reflection. "I'm not worried," he says. "I've got my daughter for the weekend."

Erica's friend lives on the river in a big Victorian with a widow's walk on the third story. The garage door is open: Lugo can see a tool bench, pegboard walls with neatly arrayed tools. Only some kind of asshole, he thinks, would keep tools so neatly arrayed. He leans over and kisses Erica on the cheek.

"I'll call in a few hours," she says, unlatching her seat belt. "You'll be home, right?"

"Finding something for your class."

He watches her walk toward the house, up the stairs. A woman steps out onto the porch and waves to Lugo and Lugo waves back.

•

What is it about the sight of a woman waving? Lugo can't go home. He can't even think about it. He drives along the riverfront, past houses he, Irene, and Erica used to point out and claim as theirs. On Saturdays they would wake up early and drive this way, looking for yard sales. The riverfront houses had the best yard sales. "How much for all of it?" Lugo would ask, and the homeowners would smile or not smile while he appraised them, waiting longer and longer each time to say he was kidding.

He barely remembers the other woman. He met her at the playground inside the mall where he used to bring Erica on the weekend. The woman was with her nephew. She and Lugo sat on a bench and watched Erica and the boy pretend to be monsters. The woman was an elementary school teacher, lonely, he could tell the minute she started talking. The sort of person who checks out books ten at a time from the library. Her plates at home were plastic, laminated over colorful drawings by her students, "Thanks for the great year, Ms. Something!" Her last name wasn't actually *Something*. Lugo can't remember her last name.

How much for all of it, he'd ask. And when he bought something, he'd ask the person selling it, "What's its story?" Just like Erica this morning. Even if it was just a belt, or an unopened picture frame. He wasn't looking for a story. He wanted them to acknowledge what they were getting rid of, to see it for the last time and perhaps feel a little regret while he handed them seventy-five cents . . .

•

Lugo drives and drives until it feels like exercise. After talking to a young woman in a booth at the mall, a woman who sold him perfume by rubbing different kinds on each wrist, asking in a woodwind voice, "So you like? They're imposters, based on designer perfumes. Can't smell the difference, right?" tilting her face close to his, and Lugo smelling something besides perfume, sweet, invigorating mall smell, after buying two bottles of perfume and telling the young woman before she handed over the receipt, "You have a great voice," and her saying thanks, and him saying, "I mean, it's studio quality," and her saying yes, tearing the receipt from the register, and him, "How old are you?" and her, unblinking, hardening her jaw, "Off you go now. Enjoy your perfumes," after walking out past the playground, driving around, reenacting the exchange in his mind, remembering it away, Lugo finds himself in a bar. It's one of those places with news clippings and snapshots of patrons covering the walls.

"It's too beautiful to be outside today," the bartender says, pouring his drink. She's the owner's wife, an older, saturnine woman whose name Lugo can never recall.

"I can only stay for one today. I have my daughter for the weekend."

The bartender drops a cardboard coaster in front of him, sets his drink atop it. "You remember Shandra, our youngest?"

"Your daughter," he says.

"Yep. We've been at it all week. Turns out last Tuesday she went and had both nipples pierced. You believe that? A stranger did it. She's nineteen, but goddamn. I said to her, 'Now why would you volunteer for that?' She says, 'A bunch of reasons.' And I say, 'One. Give me one good reason.' And she says, 'For increased pleasure, Mom.' For increased pleasure. Like she's reading it off a box."

Lugo studies the ice cubes, dissolving cavities of light, floating in his drink. "My daughter's at a birthday party."

"You could see the studs through her shirt. That's how I knew. But once they're eighteen, isn't much you can do. The cord is cut."

"Erica's just fourteen," he says. "I'm helping her with a project for school."

One drink. Lugo is gifted with willpower when he needs to be, but he rarely needs to be. He sips the drink in slow time—not too slow, he doesn't want the ice to melt—and thinks about Erica. When she was a baby, around the time of her obsession with the Popeyes sign, he, too, became obsessed: with the idea that he would die or go missing before Erica was old enough to remember him. The thought was enough to make his chest palpitate, lying in bed after a half-hour fight with Irene over something he did or failed to do, and he'd often get up to check on Erica. He would lift her out of her crib and sit in the velour glider in the corner and rock himself to sleep to the sound of her sleeping. It would take years for her to begin remembering. Like walking and talking, remembering wasn't something you were born knowing how to do.

"She's nineteen," the owner's wife says to a woman down the bar from Lugo, "but goddamn."

He takes a final sip, stands up, and starts to transition himself, mentally, home. Not to his new old apartment, he can't go there, but to his old old house, where Erica and Irene live. He needs to go there. Leaving the bar, turning the key in the ignition, driving five miles per hour below the speed limit, he tries to project casual concern. The last time he surprised Irene at home, it did not go well. She was entertaining a big group of friends, artists, some of whom Lugo had known, and she'd reluctantly invited him in and . . . it did not go well.

"We should really talk more often," he says to himself as he drives. It's a beautiful day. A few cloud wisps in an otherwise clear sky make the sky look clearer. "I think we can do better with Erica." No, too imperative. "What does Erica want for Christmas?" Close. "Is there anything Erica needs?" Closer.

•

During the winter Erica learned to walk, he brought her to the indoor playground at the mall. They went early, before the stores open, when it was just Lugo, Erica, and the mall-walkers swinging both arms in exaggerated crisscrosses to increase their heart rate. *Right behind you*, they would say, when approaching from behind. They said it in a singsong, drawing out the third syllable, to make it seem less repetitive.

This was before he met the woman who came to the playground with her nephew. The nephew was staying with her because his house was being tented and fumigated for termites. That morning she'd driven him by the house to look at the tent, she said, but the boy couldn't see it. Literally could not see it. "It's as if the tent's not there," she said. This was when Lugo knew she was lonely.

Erica was a happy baby, predictable, easy. When she didn't like what was going on, she cried. When she did, she laughed. What she liked and didn't like always made sense to Lugo.

One year, he called Popeyes corporate headquarters in Atlanta and told the customer-service woman how he and his daughter had to take the long way home from preschool so they could drive past the sign. He wanted a miniature replica of it to give to her for Christmas, but the woman said they didn't make them. Instead she sent a poster of an awestruck fat man biting into a piece of thigh meat. Beneath him, it said, "Love that chicken from Popeyes!"

By Christmas, Erica no longer cared about the sign. He drove past it a half-dozen times. "It's your sign," he would say. She wouldn't even look at it! Maybe, he thought, she was just tired of that *particular* Popeyes sign. He drove across town to a different Popeyes, stopped in front of the sign, but she remained unmoved. What was the matter with her?

"It's your *sign*," he said. He unbuckled her from her car seat and brought her into the parking lot. "Look, there, just look at it."

He lifted her chin a little too roughly and she began crying. He tried to console her. "It's okay," he said. "We'll just have to find you something new to like."

Driving home that afternoon, he felt terrible. He knew

he'd meet every phase she went through—and what did he suppose her fixation on the sign was but a phase, temporary, brief, dear—with this kind of stubbornness. Better to go out of his way to avoid the sign, better to stop keeping track.

•

At the window of the studio, behind the house, Lugo watches Irene edge a thin metal rib along a piece of greenware. Her back is to him. Her hair looks shorter than it did earlier in the day and her apron is tied in a neat bow at her back, so neat that he imagines someone helped her with it, someone careful. She shapes the corners of the pot, then crouches forward to level her gaze. She'll go on shaping it for hours before glazing it and firing it in the kiln. Next to her sits a metal caddy with four unfired pots on it. They're the color of dry chocolate, box-shaped with contoured edges, large enough to accommodate the cremains of an adult human. The thought of ending up inside a piece of Irene's pottery makes Lugo's ears perspire.

He remembers Irene, four months pregnant, ruddy and self-contained, in a state of heightened appreciativeness. Cleaning the house room by room, throwing away anything, she said, that didn't make her happy. She went on long walks by herself. She came home with her pockets full of acorns, seedpods, nutshells, leaves, all sorts of tree trash, which she would arrange artfully on their bookshelves, along the mantel. When he asked why they were there, she said, "Because they're beautiful."

He knocks on the door. She doesn't look surprised, much less pleasantly surprised, when she opens it. Her chin is streaked with slip clay. She chews on what must be a tiny piece of gum: Lugo discerns it only because he knows she can't work without it.

"Where's Erica?" she says.

He explains that he dropped her off at Adrienne's party, then went Christmas shopping at the mall where he bought a nice selection of perfume. "Do you have a minute?"

"No," she says, standing in the doorway. "I'm working. I have thirty orders to meet in the next two weeks. Why are you here?"

"I'm here to help," he says confidently. "With Erica." And he thinks: Perfect. Perfect in its timing and execution. Casual yet direct. Poised, concerned.

"You look half-cocked," she says. "You haven't shaved. You smell like a bar. You're wearing pajama bottoms."

"These?" Lugo fights the urge to look down. He watches Irene's cheeks pucker almost imperceptibly around the tiny piece of gum. "These are sweatpants, never worn these to bed. Plus I'm not even close to drunk. I haven't had a drop of scotch at all today, so." He looks down at his sweatpants—it's clear to him they're sweatpants. "Sweatpants," he repeats.

"Listen." She steps back but not away from the door. "Every time we talk about Erica, it turns into a fight. I don't want to fight anymore. Erica's fine when she's with me. I can't imagine it's all that different with you."

"She's becoming so"—Lugo looks past her inside the studio—"serious." He's searching for the rejects on their caddy, the pots she used to let him dispose of. "At least let me see what you've been working on."

"No."

How easily she dispenses that word! As if she's answering a mail-in survey about a minor appliance. Were you satisfied with our product?

The phone rings in the back of the studio. "That's the phone," she says.

"I know what a phone sounds like," Lugo says.

Irene leaves the door open while she answers it, so Lugo steps inside. "Yes," he hears her say. By her tone, instantly, unguardedly solicitous, he knows she's talking to Erica. "That's because he's standing right here." Next to the work-table are stacked four sturdy-looking green cardboard boxes with typed labels: last name comma first name. When the pots are finished, she'll pour in the contents of the boxes, seal the pots, and send them off. "Of course you're not in trouble," Irene says. Next to the green boxes is the caddy that holds the pots to be discarded, alongside the hammer with the antler handle. What's wrong with them? He lifts one of the pots from it, turns it over to see his last name, which Irene kept after they divorced—she'd already, in her words, *established herself* with it—etched on the bottom. He loves seeing it there. "I'll come do it myself," she says to Erica.

Lugo is studying a serrated scraper when she returns. "If we enjoy her childhood more," he says, "she will, too. We can't forget that."

Irene unties her apron and balls it up. "Erica's been trying to reach you for a half hour. I'm picking her up and bringing her home."

"No," Lugo says. "No, I'm going. She's mine this weekend."

"Just so you know." Irene tosses her apron onto the counter. "Erica didn't want to stay with you this weekend. She says your apartment's filthy. That you drink too much and say random things and don't take care of yourself. I made her go."

"You made her go to my house," he says. "For her own good."

"The thing *you* shouldn't forget is that it won't be long until I can't make her go anymore."

"All I know," he says, hesitating, steadying himself on the caddy, knocking one of the taller pots onto its side. It doesn't break, or if it does, it isn't audible. "Is that I'm doing everything I can."

This is not what Lugo wanted to say. It isn't true or germane, and now Irene is looking at him with undisguised pity. Sort of a smile stuck through with wires. He hates it when she employs his rhetorical patterns, uses them against him.

All I know, he wanted to say, followed by some singular insight, something that only he could know.

"I'm going," she says. "Get home. We'll hash things out later in the week."

She slopes around Lugo. He wants to switch to slow time but it's impossible with Irene. She has already started the car. She's backing out, she's miles away, she's gone. It has always been impossible.

He looks around the studio at all the artful disorder. In the back, over the slip machine, like a tub with an outboard motor, she has glued shards of old pots to the wall. He wants to pick up the pot to which she was so attentive before, so carefully shaping, and let it drop to the ground. No, this is exactly what she wants him to do. It's why she left him alone in the studio. She wants him fully unhinged. Which is probably why she told him what Erica said. She wants him hopeless.

He won't break the pot she was working on, but he can at least push the dolly into the backyard and break up the reject pots. There are three of them. Identically shaped but finished with different glazes—brown, violet, green. The special hammer is right next to them, which is how he knows they're the rejects. He pushes the dolly carefully between rows of bamboo he planted years ago, along the footpath he cut, into a clearing he made . . .

The first pot he lifts and drops. It falls with a *crunk*, breaks into four or five large pieces. Unsatisfying. The next pot he decides to break by tapping the ball peen against the side, softly, then harder, a little harder, like cracking an egg. He does this to two sides before the pot collapses into shards.

The last pot is heavier and glazed violet with a coral bead attached to the top. He lowers it to the ground and looks at it. He remembers the man in Illinois who mailed himself to freedom. If he told Erica about it on the way to the party, she would've probably thought *random random random*, but it wasn't random. It was . . . what was it?

It was integral.

This pot he wants to break with a single righteous blow of the hammer. He sets it on the ground, lifts the hammer, and strikes it once, hard. The force collapses the pot and produces a cloud of what looks like smoke, but which Lugo can see, after the cloud thins, is ash. Ash and tiny fragments of bone, which spill out onto the grass. He looks at the mess and at the hammer. He can't breathe for a long time. His first impulse is to run away, his second is to cry, but he can't do either. He can only stare at the pile for a little longer and then gather the cremains with his hands and try to sift them back into the smashed pot. Fruitless, of course, yet he tries anyway. The ashes are filled with sharp, spur-like pieces, shards of pot, shards of bone. They nip at his fingers as he drags them back and forth along the grass.

He stands up, lays the special hammer on the cart.

Lugo in normal time. All the promises and warnings and slowing down and speeding up and this is when it becomes clear. This is when he has his comeback for Irene, when he knows the thing that only he can know. He is in trouble.

english made easy

Tonight the air is cooler but not yet cold, and the houses float together and separate like boats in a bay. Lena walks alone. She is not drunk. She's had several glasses of wine, but wine doesn't seem to affect her lately. Possibly her legs are drunk. Waiting to cross the street after talking to Bern from her support group, she repeats what she said to him and it sounds perfectly sensible, perfectly sober. She said: thank you.

On Boylston, she sees old Mrs. Appleman in a yellow sweatshirt, pulling weeds. She waves Lena over to ask her name, where she lives, what her husband does for a living. Mrs. Appleman has some type of exquisitely benign dementia. She asks Lena these questions several times a week, amazed anew by each answer. "Your husband's overseas, you say?"

"He spends winters in South America. Except it's not winter there, it's summer."

"Everything's so big," Mrs. Appleman says. "The world, my house." She kneads her hands together. The backs are chafed and intricately mottled. "Which house are you again?"

Lena describes her house for Mrs. Appleman: gray with black trim, pair of jacaranda trees out front.

"I know that one," Mrs. Appleman says. She always says this. "Didn't a woman's husband die? With a baby on the way?"

Lena listens to the hollow, bone-like tock of bamboo chimes nearby. It's a mournful, an awful sound to broadcast through a neighborhood. "I've heard that, too," she says.

"Does your husband ever put his hand on your back when you walk through a doorway?" The old woman smiles and waits and, perhaps sensing Lena's unease, says, "You have such an amazed little expression. You look like you just found a lost race."

Lena pauses at each house on her way down the street. Some houses are drowsy. Some are unconditionally awake. Some are asleep. A sleeping house keeps a light going in a side window, like the dreaming part of its brain. It holds its secrets until morning.

"Visit me again soon," Mrs. Appleman said when Lena left. "Knock on my door if I'm not out here. Talk to me, fertilize me, make sure I'm still alive."

Lena approaches her own house. From the sidewalk she watches the babysitter pace back and forth with Lyle asleep on her shoulder. She's wearing a telephone earpiece, which she speaks into like a gerbil lapping at a water pipe. Lena suspects the babysitter tries to breastfeed Lyle. It's not a heartfelt suspicion, but once, when Lena returned home early, the babysitter's shirt was inside out. The babysitter said she was worried that the baby would spit up on her while she rocked him to sleep. She pulled off her shirt right there and put it on correctly and Lena stared at the cross pendant nestled reverently in the babysitter's tidy cleavage. Jesus looked so snug there, hardly suffering at all.

After a few minutes, the babysitter sits down on the sofa, out of view, and Lena continues up her street, toward the bigger homes.

She's supposed to be at her group meeting, but she can't do it tonight. She tried. She stood in the lobby of the community center and hesitated at the directory: Alcoholics Anonymous, Overeaters Anonymous. Lena's group was at the bottom. Seeing the name, Parents Without Partners, made her feel sick. So grave and frivolous. It brought to mind hopeless moms groping through the opening notes of a song for men to waltz with. Lena would've preferred to enlist with the alcoholics, the overeaters, anything but the partnerless parents. At her first meeting, the group sat in a circle and took turns introducing themselves.

"I'm Lena," she said when it was her turn. "I have a seven-month-old boy. His father died, on his horse—he was an equestrian. Both were killed in an equestrian accident. The horse's name was Diamonds. It's nice to be here."

This is how it goes for Lena. Start with a lie, tell more lies in service of the original lie, until she begins to resent herself, and those she lied to—especially those she lied to—for the lies. People, she's come to realize since Andrew died, ask too many questions, and they're never the right questions.

Earlier tonight, while sneaking away from the community center, she ran into Bern, whose wife was killed after kids dropped rocks from a highway overpass onto the windshield of her car. He called out to Lena, "Forget something?"

"Yes," she said. "I just remembered I can't make it, unfortunately. I've been invited to a costume party."

"Fun," Bern said, catching up with her. Though he wore a tie, crisply knotted, Lena sensed he was unemployed. She sensed he hung around a park all day trying to get people to do things against their will. "Where's your costume?"

"It's at home," Lena said. "Drying."

"Drying," he repeated, turning it over to show the absurdity of it. "I'd like to go to a party. I can't remember the last time I was at—"

"I'd invite you," she interrupted, "but I'm just going for a few minutes. You know. In and out, that's me. Quickety-quick. Now you see me, now you don't."

"Sounds like someone's been celebrating early."

"Thank you," she said. She didn't realize what he was alluding to until halfway down the block, looking in on her neighbor's houses. But she wasn't drunk. She was safely housed, immunized against sadness. "Thank you," she repeated while waiting to cross the street.

Andrew never put his hand on her back when they walked through a doorway. He never called her anything but Lena. Sometimes they would hold hands on the armrest at the movies. It was a way of being simultaneously together and alone, the best way to be.

Houses at night are open books. She need only stand in a front yard for a minute to know what they are about. There are stories of love and marriage and severance, there are coming-of-age stories. Most are predictable, lackluster. Some foretell endings so forlorn—derelict sprinkler head, yawning garage door—that Lena has to hurry past to the next house and the next.

It's been almost a year. She doesn't keep track, she won't check her calendar, but she knows. Often Andrew's sister calls from St. Pete to tell Lena things. "He used to follow me and my friends all around," she says. "He tried to hide, but I could see him over the bushes. I didn't care. When I picture him now he's on a couch with a candy cane, and there's marble tile and he's barefoot. He was a big fan of candy canes, Lena. Know that. He ate them year-round."

Lena can hear an ice tray cracking and a glass being refilled. She's pretty sure the sister has written things down and is reading from a card.

"Lena's turn," the sister says. "Tell me something I don't know."

He died on a Friday. He collapsed while riding his bike to the post office to drop off a stack of misdelivered letters addressed to S. T. Valeric, the former owner of the house, who apparently was in some kind of club that involved young Asian women sending him letters. The letters, some of which she and Andrew opened and read, often contained specific physical measurements and a list of sexually tinged likes and dislikes. "I like animal of all kind," one woman wrote. "Sometime I dream of riding me nude a Black Beauty."

Fridays, Andrew would return the letters to the post office. He enjoyed making rituals out of tiny events like this.

He cut his cheek when he fell off his bike, after a rupture

in his heart. By the time Lena made it to the hospital, he was dead. The first thing she noticed was the cut, and even after the doctor described exactly what had happened, pointing to his own chest to demonstrate, after a woman, a nurse not dressed as a nurse, asked if she'd like a sedative and Lena said, "I can't, I'm having a baby," which made her cry and cry until she blacked out and woke up with an IV in her arm and there was Andrew's sister—she was still thinking about that cut on his cheek.

A houseful of people for the funeral and then an empty house and a freezer full of stews. Lena became adept at bundling up her unhappiness, sealing it, shipping it from sight. She focused on the thing inside her due in five months. She determined not to poison him with even the merest drop of sadness. The pregnancy would be a five-month ride for the baby in a car built for one. They'd sing songs. They'd head west, away from nightfall, ahead of the retreating sun. She went to the store and bought baby slippers, fleece blankets, a book called *What to Expect When You're Expecting*. He lived in a womb, she'd tuck herself into one, too.

He was born on a Monday, a quick delivery fogged by pain. The first few months, he slept next to her in bed and she woke up every twenty minutes to make sure he wasn't suffocating beneath covers, or choking on a screw that had come loose from, say, the ceiling fan and dropped down next to him on the bed.

She's ready now, ready to mourn. She wasn't fully successful at delaying it while pregnant. She broke down while reading cards from their friends, while cleaning out his desk, after waking from particularly convincing dreams. They're vicious, those dreams, sharper than any memory she can summon. Sharper than any photograph. The grief's still there, somewhere. Every so often she'll brush against its thorny surface and she knows it's waiting, existing separately from her, growing.

"I can't think of anything right now," she says to Andrew's sister. "Let's talk about something else."

"Something else? What's there else to talk about? Recipes? The government?"

"I don't know," Lena says. "Anything."

Andrew's sister sighs. Ice cubes clack against glass.

"Is the baby busy?" she says. "If you aren't gonna talk about anything at least put Lyle on the phone for a minute."

Lyle rests on a nursing pillow in her lap. His eyes open and close, open and close. "He's almost asleep," Lena says. "He's right here."

"Just put the phone to his ear real quick. I won't be long."

She should have said it the other way: *He's right here, he's almost asleep.* Andrew's sister breathes and waits. What the hell. Lena holds the phone to Lyle's ear and watches his face shudder and awaken as Andrew's sister tells him things.

Lena, careful Lena, pushing Lyle, bundled in his stroller under a purple fleece, around the block. She stops to talk to her neighbors. They know about Andrew, but they won't mention him. Maybe they think she's forgotten and they're hesitant to remind her. Their sympathy has dissolved and reconstituted as intense interest in the baby. What a terrific head of hair! they say, kneeling to fully acknowledge him. What nice soft full healthy pleasing miraculous hair. And those eyes—wait, he's smiling! He's beautiful, a dead ringer for his mother, they say.

Lena knows they're being dishonest. She's become sallow-eyed, crow-like, cagey. A new girl at the salon cut her hair too short and now, hiding under a sweatshirt hood, she looks like a medieval lesbian. She sees only Andrew in the baby's unresolved contours. The baby looks like Andrew.

He's asleep now, she can tell without looking at him. She has to be outdoors. She has to keep walking. Past other people's houses and bird feeders made out of two-liter bottles and landscapers sterilizing their saws and sprinkling powdered fox urine around the bases of palms, to ward off moles.

She finds Mrs. Appleman push-brooming sweet-gum husks from the sidewalk in front of her house. Her face is red from exertion, her hair tied back with a gold ribbon in a perfectly uniform bow.

"A baby!" she says. "Nothing in the world's better than a

baby." She peeks into Lyle's stroller, reaches under the blanket. "What a beauty." On the crown of his skull, a diamond-shaped soft spot pits and puffs with his heartbeat. "What a nice warm fortune cookie."

Mrs. Appleman asks Lena her name, the baby's name, what her husband does for a living, where they live. "I know that house," she says. "There was a woman who died there? Or had a baby who died?"

"They all died." Lena studies the fallow grooves in Mrs. Appleman's face. Every expression she's ever had, every smile and glower and scowl, is intimated there. Conveying an expression now seems a matter of animating certain premade wrinkles. "We live there now," she says.

Mrs. Appleman stands up, gives the sidewalk a stiff final sweep. "So unlucky." She lets the broom fall into the grass. "You can tell the unlucky ones, you can always tell."

She bends down again, over the baby. Lena wonders if there's even a glint of recognition in Mrs. Appleman, if she ever notices that she's reliving a continuous single day. How awful it is to be consigned to this, Lena thinks. And what a blessing not to notice it, and how awful.

"How can you tell?" Lena asks.

"How can you tell what, sweetheart?"

Lena feels a shiver like a thumbnail sketching letters up her back.

"If someone's unlucky."

Mrs. Appleman makes faces at the baby, squinting and

curling her bottom lip over her top lip. "How about you start talking right now?" she says to Lyle. "I'll put a dime in your mouth and you tell my future." She grips his socked foot like a lever. "Babies are the nicest, especially real babies. But they're sad, too. But they're also nice. Nice and sad."

Lyle has opened his eyes but he hasn't yet awoken. Mrs. Appleman leans into his stroller like the last swaying tentacle of a dream.

"I'm going to kiss him in case I don't see him again," she says.

Lena pushes the stroller up Boylston, lifting the front wheels over oak roots that have ripped through the sidewalk, before realizing she's a half-block from the post office, near the spot where Andrew died. She doesn't turn around. The post office is a two-story whitewashed building, just a building. As she walks past, she notices a bike with side baskets and a laughing cow sticker on the crossbar, locked to a bike rack. She stops and stares at it. Chain, sprocket, and spokes are rusted, both tires are flat. She wonders who took the time to move it out of the road. The lock is a cheap combination lock, a chain sleeved in green plastic. The ambulance driver? Lena doesn't know what to do. She finds herself nearing the bike, patting her hand on the seat. Lifting the lock, turning the tumbler—the combination is 0525, Lena's birthday. She unhooks the chain and drops it into one of the bike's baskets.

"Go now," she says. "Off with you."

It seems unfair that people should leave behind so much

noise. Not a single discernible sound but patches of cracking static to mark where they were.

If bikes were horses, Lena thinks, stealing one last look at it. She leaves the thought incomplete, lets it grow untended, like a deep-woods weed, as she pushes Lyle home.

•

She meets Andrew's sister at an outlet mall in Kissimmee. The mall is exactly midway between their houses, Andrew's sister has calculated. She brings her husband, Cal, who has a different job every time Lena sees him. Currently, he cold-calls people and tries to get them to buy water softeners.

"It's incredible," the sister says. "He picks up the phone, dials a number, introduces himself, and pretty soon *he's* the one answering questions. Telling them about aquifers and sodium content and problem stains."

"I've always been tuned to a certain longing in other people," Cal says sadly. "I can touch it, I can massage it in place, but I can't do nothing else with it. I hate being a salesman."

"He suffers from an excess of empathy," Andrew's sister says. "And several other things."

"You ever feel like you've mishandled your talents?" he asks Lena. He doesn't wait for an answer. "I do. I feel like mine got dumped out and put back in the wrong containers. Did Beth tell you that we're in counseling because she caught me making love to a puppet?"

Beth is Andrew's sister. "Wait," Lena says, confused. "An actual puppet?"

"As actual as they get, I guess. It was just a little old hand puppet, an owl. Nothing perverted."

"It was a gift for someone," Beth says. Then, to Cal: "Why don't you go over to the toys and find something nice for Lyle."

The three of them are walking the aisles of a store where all the items are slightly irregular or damaged. Windbreakers with slight tears along the sleeve, board games missing pieces. Some of the things you have to pick up and examine before you can tell what's wrong with them, and even then Lena isn't always sure. She and Andrew's sister never buy anything. They come to follow the blue tape line on the floor that marks off how far they've walked, around and around the store, until they've gone two miles.

"He wasn't making love," Beth says after Cal's gone. "And that's not even one of the top five reasons we're in counseling."

Lyle's at home with the sitter. He woke up five times last night. Lena finally gave up and brought him to bed with her so she could nurse him while she slept. On these sleepless nights, her waking-mind and her dream-mind merge and all of her days with Andrew contract to one day. Morning, noon, night: when she wakes up the next morning, he's gone.

"How go the meetings?" Andrew's sister asks her. "Are they helping?"

"Fine," Lena says. They walk past a woman trying on a pair of brown terry shorts over her jeans. "Actually, not fine. I've missed the past few. They sort of make me want to unpack my brain when I get home, set it on a cutting board, and chop it in half like a roast chicken. It seemed like the men were there just to pick up women."

"How pathetic. I bet most of them aren't even widowed. I can imagine them trying to work up the tears by thinking about childhood dogs. Tell me if they bother you, and I'll get Cal on the phone with them. He's protective of you, you know. Behind the scenes."

Most of Lena's lies are fatigue lies, convincing details pinch-hitting for less convincing ones. She knew the bit about men at the meetings would explain everything to Andrew's sister.

"Let's go on a trip together," Beth says. "Me and you."

"That sounds nice," Lena says without thinking.

"I don't mean *nice*. I'm not talking about sightseeing. I mean the desert, someplace with hostile plants and extreme weather and animals that want to kill us. The Southwest, Mexico. I've got guidebooks. Mexicans have a much more honest relationship with the dead than we do, Lena. We can learn from them. We can go to shrines. We don't need a vacation. We need the kind of a place that'll scour us raw."

Lena's trying to concentrate on walking, the scissor of her arms, the listless momentum of her legs. If she fell down right now, she would not get up for a while. Her fellow shoppers would have to tend to her in front of the bin of mother-of-pearl picture frames, on the side of which is a handwritten sign: MAKE MEMORIES AN OCCASION FOR CELEBRATION!

"I don't want another honeymoon," she says.

Beth is glaring at her, Lena can tell without looking. She doesn't know why Beth keeps calling her and asking her to meet. They weren't friends when Andrew was alive. He almost never talked about his sister, actually, something Lena reminds herself whenever she feels her memory of him being overlaid by Beth's, clarified, stunted, retraced in crayon.

"Will you just talk to me?" Beth says after a while. "Sing, tell a joke, yell at me, punch me in the stomach. Shit. I'm dying here."

"I've been gathering pictures and stories to make a book about him," Lena says. "A scrapbook, for Lyle when he grows up."

Beth sighs. Lena isn't sure if Beth's exasperated or relieved. "That is so perfect," she says. "Listen, I want to help with this. I can do all the chapters before you guys met. The Early Years."

"Sure," Lena says. "There's no way I can do this alone."

A scrapbook. Lena looks over her shoulder at the bins and shelves to figure out where the idea came from. Other people walking the blue-lined circuit approach and say, "On your left," then walk past. Not all lies are lies, she thinks. Some lies are wishes, some are just-born plans.

As they leave the store, they find Cal sitting out front in

an oversize wooden chair with rubber electrodes against his temples. Bulbs along the top of the chair light up every few seconds and Cal jerks and twitches around in the chair as if he's being electrocuted. Old Sparky, the chair's called. Three minutes for a quarter.

"What's it feel like?" a little girl asks him between jolts.

"Horrible," Cal says. "I'm trying to commit to one last thought before I die, something lofty. But the chair won't let me. All I can think is, 'My God, I am currently being executed.'"

A plastic shopping bag rests near Cal's bound feet. Lena can see the box inside: Bedtime Zoo Mobile.

"Just picture the two of us in the desert," Beth says to Lena. "Surviving. Realizing things."

At home, Lena finds the babysitter asleep on the couch. Her telephone earpiece is askew and there are crinkle marks on her face and neck from the corduroy pillow. Lena imagines someone on the other end singing a lullaby.

Upstairs, Lyle is in his crib. Lena sits in the rocking chair and assembles the zoo-animal mobile. When she's done, she holds it above him, turns it on, and watches it rotate at approximately half speed. Its once-happy jingle has slowed to a glum dirge. The giraffes and elephants look confused, swiveling above Lyle. He sleeps on his back with his hands behind his head, aggressively at ease in the world. Lena switches off the mobile and kisses Lyle without kissing him.

On the edge of sleep, the threads of the day unravel in her mind and she stirs awake to retie them. She makes bows of the loose strands, admires the bows, and watches them unravel again.

•

She buys a blank book and rubber cement and sheets of hard-stock paper for descriptions and whatever else she might write. She buys photo corner tabs. She buys an exceptionally nice pen in a plastic casket. She realizes she's just indulging Andrew's sister and herself, but it doesn't bother her. In fact, the preparations are strangely consoling. It's as if she's assembling an alibi. When Andrew's sister calls, she knows exactly what to tell her.

Andrew's sister calls. Lena's napping on the couch with Lyle sprawled across the crook of her arm. She ignores the phone until the ringing dies, and then it awakens a few seconds later and rings again. Zombie rings, Lena thinks. Her shoulder and arm are asleep and moist with sweat.

"Listen to this," Beth says. Lena listens to the angry cracking of ice cubes being freed from their tray. She waits for it to stop, waits for Lyle to start stirring on her lap. Then there's a click and Lena hears two children's voices, a boy and a girl. They're arguing about what to watch on TV and pretty soon the boy's yelling at the girl: "Watch what you want! Watch what you want!"

Another click and Beth comes on the line. "It's him, it's

Andrew. I used to hide a tape recorder and then start an argument, and play it back afterward. He hated it."

"What a terrible thing to do to somebody," Lena says.

"That isn't the point of my story, Lena. I'm finding all kinds of loot like this in my attic. It'll be perfect for the book." A sip and a colossal swallow. Lena's mouth is suddenly dry. She lays Lyle on the couch, sets her nursing pillow next to him so he doesn't fall off, and goes into the kitchen. She pours a glass of wine while Andrew's sister tells her about all the things she found in her attic: tapes, drawings, letters, photographs.

Lena, too, went through a box of her pictures the other day, after which she put them on the highest shelf in the house. So many pictures. It was as if she knew something bad was going to happen, overdocumenting their past together to augur her togetherless future. Look here, remember this. She wishes she were a druid, or an ancient Eskimo, someone with a past that's an unbroken slur of labor and meals and darkness and seasons and fires. None of the pictures are real. They don't capture anything as it happened or as she remembers it happening. They're just pictures of people having their pictures taken.

"Good or bad, he was always himself," Beth says. "We need to make sure we show that in our book."

"I'm writing it down right now," Lena says, pouring another glass of wine. "He . . . was . . . always . . . himself."

"All right then. I gotta go get Cal from the stupid chiropractor. Can I talk to Lyle real quick?"

Lena looks over at Lyle, still asleep on the couch. "Here he is," she says. She covers the phone receiver with her hand. Andrew's sister begins humming softly, a little raspily. She doesn't speak. The ice chimes against the side of her glass. Lena can hear crying, as soft and melodic as the humming. Beth says, "What are people supposed to do all day?"

●

The community center, a converted mansion with terrazzo floors, smells like crushed gardenias. Lena peeks into rooms, nods to the alcoholics cradling Styrofoam cups and looking like hollow owls, nods to a group of women who are clapping. They clap until Lena is halfway up the stairs. They stop, but her thought, that maybe this is a support group for people who can't quit clapping, continues. She holds it with her until she is seated, filled with dread, waiting for her own meeting to begin.

The wine seems to have electrified the blood in her legs. Concentrating, she can feel the pressurized suck and surge of each artery and vein. She closes her eyes and *sees* it, lit up in blue and red like a transit map.

She doesn't recognize any of the dozen or so other part-nerless parents—unsurprising, since she hasn't been to a meeting in more than a month. Tonight, a bald younger man stands up and begins: "Hello. My name is Todd."

One by one, the others in the room repeat, "Hello. My name is," and then fill in their names. Name tags and markers are passed around. Lena writes her name on the tag and sticks it on the breast pocket of her blouse.

Todd walks over to an older Asian woman clutching a rolled-up newspaper in her lap and says, "Good evening." And the woman says, "Guh evening." He says, "The evening. Is good." And the woman says, "The evening, it's guh." He repeats this with everyone else in the room, including Lena. He tells them that he is American and they tell him what they are: Chinese, Ecuadorian, Ghanaian, Chinese. Lena says Albanian. The teacher tells them what he ate for dinner and they tell him what they ate for dinner—almost everyone ate exactly what the teacher ate.

Lena nods whenever he looks her way. She should leave, but she doesn't want to appear rude. After she drinks several glasses of wine, the feelings of strangers seem like something she'll be called to account for. Plus she's starting to enjoy listening to her classmates earnestly tiptoe through the rudiments of conversation, and to partake in it herself. It's like praying. The hope of simple acquisition, the guarantee that she won't be asked any question she can't answer.

"I like my friends," Todd says. "I like baseball. What do you like?"

One by one, they tell the teacher what they like. They like tea, ice cream, springer spaniel, church, bedroom, friends, English, sister, sailboat, Cadillac Seville, breakfast.

Lena is last. "What do *you* like?" he asks her.

"I like horses," she says. "I like walking and most flowers. I like the feeling of somebody whispering really close to my ear."

"Outstanding!" he says. "I *love* my wife and daughter. I *love* our Lord and Savior Jesus Christ. What do *you* love, Lena?"

His small, small eyes study her. He's trying to look warm and attentive but his eyes won't allow it. They're the eyes of a creature that needs to detect only if prey is moving toward him or away.

"I love everything I like," she says. "Plus Twix bars. And puppies."

"Okay," he says less enthusiastically. He claps twice and just as he's about to move to the next person, he turns to Lena and says, "This is English Made Easy. It sounds like you should be in one of the advanced classes. Or one of the recovery groups."

She looks at the rowdy array of faces: five other women, some young, some old, some smiling, some not, unpretty. A man next to her winks as he holds a plastic water bottle a few inches from his mouth and squeezes out a stream.

"I was waiting for a break to leave," she says. "I must've miscounted as I was walking from the stairwell. I didn't want to interrupt."

"Now's the perfect time," he says. "The time. Is now perfect." Up close, she perceives in him something begging to be cut and sprung. It makes her cold. He waves a bulbous hand

{177}

too close to her face. "Bye-bye, Lena. Everyone say good-bye to Lena."

Everyone says good-bye with more enthusiasm than anyone's ever said good-bye to her. Many of them wave.

"Have a safe trip," he says.

"Have a safe trip," the class says.

She stands and quickly walks to the door. "I'm not going on a trip. You don't have to turn it into a big lesson. Lena isn't going on a trip," she says to the class. "Lena's just leaving."

Todd laughs a meaningless laugh. "Lena was in the wrong room," she hears him say as she closes the door. "Lena was not in the correct room." Everyone else repeats, "Lena was in the wrong room. Lena was not in the correct room."

She sits on a bus bench in front of the community center, crying for the first time in weeks, covering her face with her hands, mashing the tears back into her eyes. She stays there for a while. Whenever she feels like she might be finished, she pictures herself walking away from the meeting, the class saying, *Lena was not in the correct room*, and it revives her. She could have said that her husband had a rupture in his heart—his heart. Had a rupture—filled a Ziploc bag with water and dropped it on the floor to show the meaning of the word *rupture*. She could've told them she had a new baby and she was waiting to explain everything to the baby so she could explain it to herself. Once upon a time, two people were talking and then one of them left on his bike to go to the post office and then he was gone. Taking a big pill from her pocket, holding it up, and swallowing it to show them what gone was.

A bus stops in front of the bench. The driver opens the door. "I'm not going anywhere," Lena says. She stands, wipes her eyes.

"You don't have to leave," he says, studying her over a pair of bifocals. "Slow night. I was just making sure you was okay."

I'm fine, she says. Benches, she says, they always make me sad.

The driver nods kindly and says something about benches. As he drives off, Lena imagines herself having boarded the bus, so now there are two Lenas, one on the bus and one walking around her neighborhood, again, slowing down in front of lighted houses but not stopping. Along the horizon, the sky is purplish at the lower edges, darker directly above. The sky is deeper there, Lena thinks. If you were going to dive in, this would be where you'd do it.

The other Lena rides through the city, careless, studying herself in a compact mirror. The other Lena quickly comes to an untroubled consensus about her reflection. She is pretty, not flawless but pretty enough to outpace whatever might befall her, lapping it again and again.

Mrs. Appleman is sitting at the base of a pair of date palms in her front yard, tearing bread crusts and throwing them to a pair of squirrels on the sidewalk. "Look how desperate they are," she says to Lena. The squirrels inch closer to Mrs. Appleman, then scamper back, startled, when she throws the crusts, then again move toward her once they've finished eating. "Those greedy faces remind me of something."

"How's your night going, Mrs. Appleman?"

She tilts her head to the side, pausing to consider the question. Lena imagines a thought sliding and slowly melting, like butter across a hot pan, toward the fogged bottom half of Mrs. Appleman's mind. Liquefied upon arrival. "Fair to good, I'd say. How about yours, Lena?"

Lena. That word, uttered so often earlier in the community center, echoes on the inside walls of her chest. It slaps her awake. "Do you remember me?"

"I remember everyone," Mrs. Appleman says, underhanding a crust over the heads of the squirrels. "A man came to my house years ago, offered to buy these two palms here for five hundred dollars. He said he could just dig them up and haul them away for me. I'd never heard such a thing. Ever since then, I look around my neighborhood and I can tell who's been selling their trees. Everyone. I'm probably the only one left."

Lena feels a door slowly closing. She tries to wait for Mrs. Appleman to finish feeding the squirrels, but a third and fourth squirrel have joined the original two, and Mrs. Appleman continues throwing the crusts to the same squirrel, probably the first one to arrive, and the others won't go near him.

"My husband died last year," Lena says. "I have a baby, a boy. We live in that gray-and-black house down the street."

Mrs. Appleman looks at her, tilting her head again. "I know that house. Was he the one buying the trees?"

No, Lena says. She describes Andrew. He was a teacher. They met in the checkout line of a supermarket. He wrote his phone number on a box of Chicken in a Biskit. They eloped, had a courthouse wedding, honeymooned in the Keys. Then he died while riding his bike to the post office. Facts. Nothing not true. "I'm still saving things to tell him," she says. "I think that's one of my problems."

Though Mrs. Appleman makes little affirmative sounds while listening, it's impossible to make out any single expression on her face. So thoroughly and intricately wrinkled, it appears animated by several expressions—happiness, sorrow, surprise, pity, reluctance, hope—at once.

Lena says, "You know when you're on the phone and the other person's line goes dead? But you keep talking and after a while you say *hello hello* and there's no answer? I know I need to get myself going again, move on, move away, move up, whatever you're supposed to do."

"You came over and visited me before, didn't you? With a baby."

"Lyle," Lena says. "That's us."

"Of course," Mrs. Appleman says. "The looker. That's the kind of baby stays with you when he's gone. He puts his little hand into your mouth, pulls out your fortune, and makes it his own." She turns her bread bag inside out and dumps the crumbs on the grass in front of her. She hands Lena the empty bag and says, "It's late. I need to be out here in my yard but you should go home and take care of that boy. He better not be all alone."

"I'm going," Lena says.

Heading up Boylston, she studies the houses next to Mrs. Appleman's. Their motion-activated porch lights turn on when she walks by. At certain hours, houses talk in their sleep, forgiving their occupants for the injuries of the day. In single file, unspeaking, each day stands next to the ones before it and after it. She and Andrew met in the morning, fell in love in the afternoon, and were married in the evening. Tomorrow he will be gone. Facts. Nothing not true. Tomorrow he'll be everywhere.

She doesn't go home. She circles the block, turns right turns right turns right, and finds herself back at Mrs. Appleman's. The old woman hasn't moved from the base of the date palm. She looks up, smiles, and waves when she sees Lena approaching.

"When we were talking," Lena says, "I was still trying to figure out how I was going to explain it to him when I get home. What to leave out and what to include."

"Him who, sweetheart?"

"Andrew. The man we were just talking about."

Mrs. Appleman squints at Lena. It's fully night now. Her front yard is illuminated by a pair of floodlights above the garage. "Lena," she says, staring at Lena's chest straight to her drab organs.

"That's me. Remember Lyle?"

"Lena. L-E-N-A." She taps out the letters on Lena's chest, just below her clavicle. Lena looks down and sees the name tag from the meeting. "What brings you out on this big dark night?"

No recognition, just a smiling reserve. Lena can't believe it. She's been gone for five minutes at the most. She wants to grip Mrs. Appleman by the shoulders and shake her and say, "How can you not remember?"

The old woman's face is besieged by happiness. Each moment for her exists singly, like a nest, or an island, or a song. "I knew someone named Lena," she says. "It's nice to finally meet another." She raises her arm to suggest a vast space. "This is my neighborhood."

the big finish

Everyone on the ship calls Hayes the birdman, except for the birds, who call him Ned. Ned must have been the name of the ship's previous birdman, because Hayes's name is Hayes. The birds say it with a Dixie accent: *Nay-ed.* The previous birdman taught them some nasty habits and Hayes doesn't know enough about birds to unteach them. He knows very little about birds actually. He applied for a job as a line cook, and when the recruiter asked about his previous experience working in a dog-grooming van years ago, he explained it was one of the most worthwhile things he'd ever done.

"I wasn't just clipping dogs," Hayes told him in the man's office. "I was changing how they felt about themselves. Dogs can't talk, of course, but during that final brushing, their expression would be like, 'I am not the same dog.' "

The recruiter scribbled into his notepad—Hayes calculated by the intensity of the scribbling that he was doing either very poorly or very well. The man asked Hayes what he knew about birds.

"Well," Hayes said, "I know I could spend the rest of my life admiring their liberty, their proud majesty. I know their pull is ancient."

Hayes, still living in the small college town he moved to after high school, had been feeling, but not acting, his age. He was thirty-five, a rundown version of himself at age twenty. He needed out. He needed, he decided the moment the recruiter brought up the birds, to be traveling on a commercial cruise liner around the island-littered Caribbean, performing poolside with two African gray parrots. And maybe a business card that said simply: T. R. HAYES, SHOWMAN.

"Majesty," the recruiter repeated. "I like that."

"I've also worked with rabbits," Hayes said. He hadn't put the rabbits on his résumé. He'd been trying to forget the rabbits. "And mice." He'd been trying to forget the mice, too.

The recruiter scribbled even more ardently. Hayes was doing really well! Or really poorly! When the recruiter was finished, he said, "You seem like a man equipped to appreciate the unusual needs of our birds."

And Hayes was, he is. Under the right conditions, he can muster enthusiasm toward just about anything. Birds, spiders, turtlenecks, olives. He's been working on the ship for almost six months. He entertains kids. He smiles and says hello to everyone he makes eye contact with. He lugs his personality around like milk in a big open pail, sloshing it all over the place. It's one of the discount cruise liners, advertised in the free newspaper. Stakes are agreeably low.

"I am the birdman," he tells a group of children gathered on the sundeck, "and these are my birds, Chick and Tara. I wasn't always the birdman. Before the birds I worked with dogs and I was the dogman; before dogs, it was rabbits, and I was the rabbitman; before the rabbits, *mice* . . ."

His manner is untilled, vaguely Ottoman. He washes his hands constantly and this morning there are two wet marks on the front of his pants, one large, one small: a planet and its moon.

"Come, come closer," he says, and the children step forward. Their faces remind him of expensive bicycles left unlocked. What's he doing? Hayes doesn't always know. He tries to startle the children more than he bores, but he doesn't want to mar them. Irina's first rule of working with children: Do not mar. But Hayes has trouble gauging his effect. Their open, solicitous faces, their anticipation—he's tempted to alarm them with things that are loud and untrue. To say, for instance, "Kids, it would be an honor to make love to all of your aunts and great-aunts and mothers, one by one, on a picnic table. Even the very old ones. Afterward I would have a special trophy made, to look at when the time comes and I'll never again have the volition to make love on a picnic table."

Irina's second, third, and fourth rules of working with children: Refrain, refrain, refrain. Irina is Hayes's boss.

He says, "I need to tell you kids something incredible. Chick and Tara, their wings aren't clipped. They could fly away right now if they wanted, but they'd rather stay here to entertain you."

The children study the birds, Chick on the left and Tara on the right. Their feathers are rose-petal soft and their compact bodies are ashy-gray, darkening to black in their faces, as if something foul and heavy is concentrated there. Because the birds are so uneager to entertain, every show is different and exactly the same. Today, well before the finale, the children grow bored and wander off to the kiddie pool to watch an obese shirtless man with chest pains having his blood pressure taken.

Do not stop the show. Another Irina rule. Even if no one is watching, continue like you're performing at the Met to a crowd of all the people who've ever wronged you or doubted you or failed to grasp crucial aspects of your personality.

"The big finish!" Hayes says, and Chick and Tara take flight, ascend, and orbit the ship, twenty yards portside and twenty yards starboard. It still gives him a queasy thrill. When they return and alight on their spruce post, Hayes sees resignation in their cracked eyes. He feels resignation himself, feels it like a kite string dangling above his stretched hand. They could easily fly off to St. Croix, Cuba, Dominica to live like dignitaries among fruit groves, but here they are. They say, and he has no reason not to believe them, apart from the fact that he doesn't believe them, that they'd miss him.

"That's our show, kids," he says, loud enough for them to hear him at the kiddie pool. The shirtless man is being given a bottle of water now. Some of the kids are clapping for him. Hayes unlatches the cage and Chick and Tara toddle inside.

"Ned," Tara says. "Poor poor Ned."

"Our man," Chick says. "Loyal Ned. Courage. Striking."

"Hayes," he tells the birds. "Can you say *Hayes*? Ned's long gone, he hasn't worked here in months. He went back to junior college to study small-engine repair. Do you understand? He left you to spend time with small engines."

"Ned won't leave," Tara says. "Blood Ned. Roots."

"Here." He dumps a giant Ziploc of honeydew into their cage. "Have a treat." The birds loudly devour the honeydew as he wheels them back to their cabin, thankful, silent, thankfully silent.

After the show, he and the birds are supposed to have forty-five minutes alone together every day. Meaningful contact, the instruction manual calls it, which means him sitting shirtless on the bed in his cabin, telling Chick and Tara about himself while they scrutinize him from their massive cage.

Hayes approached the assignment earnestly at first. He liked the job and aimed to keep it. He told the birds about his childhood, about college. He described his former jobs. He started with the dogs.

He told them about a Seeing Eye dog named Nimbus he once groomed. When he was done, the owner, a woman in her thirties, said, "Well, that's the sorriest haircut I've ever seen." Hayes apologized—maybe she was only partially blind—but she said she was joking. She invited him inside and showed everything Nimbus could do. He could turn lights off and on, and could work the ceiling-fan remote; he even barked when the oven was finished preheating.

The blind woman was not unattractive, Hayes explained to the birds. She had gray eyes with white whites. She wore a matching blue outfit and Hayes concocted a scenario where the woman tried on different clothes and Nimbus barked when she found ones that matched. Maybe he really liked a certain shirt and would pretend it matched when it didn't. Hayes imagined Nimbus enjoyed seeing her in her under-wear, so he let her go through six or seven outfits before barking. But didn't the woman know dogs were color-blind? Or that he just wanted to see her in her underwear? Hayes felt sorry for her until he remembered that it was his fantasy, and then he felt sorry for himself.

While Hayes talked, the birds preened themselves in the mirror attached to their cage, seemingly ignoring him. Their cage, multitiered and filled with ropes and beads, took up nearly half of his cabin, which was why he was permitted to room alone, sort of alone.

The blind woman, Hayes continued, then asked if he would cut *her* hair. He said he hadn't been trained to cut human hair, but she insisted. He brought her and Nimbus into the unit—this is what they called the dog-grooming van, the *unit*—cut her bangs, trimmed an inch off the back. Looking at Nimbus, Hayes saw his haircut was indeed sorry. Hanks of hair on his legs, fur between his paws. He wore a vest with a patch that said DON'T PET ME, I'M WORKING.

Hayes visited the blind woman many times after that. Whenever they made love, Nimbus began to bark, as if Hayes might be injuring her. "It's okay!" she yelled from under him. "It's okay! It's okay!" It was sort of off-putting. Soon she had to shut Nimbus in the laundry room before they went to her bedroom, but he barked anyway, quick distant lurching barks like a werewolf's heartbeat.

"She was remarkable," he told the birds. "She used her hands as eyes. I still think about her all the time."

"Enough, Ned," the bigger bird, Chick, said. "Make it night now."

This was the first time he'd heard either of them speak. He thought it might be a canned phrase, something they used in the show.

Tara lifted one of her talons to her mouth, delicately chewed a black nail. She said, "Rub out. Retreat. Smolder. Make it night."

Hayes found the cover and slipped it over their cage. He lay down listening to what he first took to be steady, sleepful breathing. He listened and listened until he had no doubt: the birds were whispering to each other.

"The laundry room," he heard one of them repeat. "The laundry room."

•

Often, very often lately, Hayes has the urge to run around the ship yelling, "Man overboard! Man overboard!" The budget-cruise-goers are so fearless and serene. All they care about is finding out what time the midnight buffet is, or what the complimentary daiquiris cost. Near the pool, men tee up golf balls and drive them into the ocean. Wind-crazed gulls trail the ship toward deeper water. "No land in sight!" he wants to yell. They need to be snatched from their stupor. They need to remember a time when an open sea *meant* something.

Hayes doesn't run around yelling, "Man overboard!"

He's required to smile and say hello to any guest he makes eye contact with. It's become a game: staring guests down, begging them to look at him, so he can smile and say hello.

Today Irina, the children's activities coordinator, comes to see his show. Quality control. Irina is a thick, officious Dutchwoman in drugstore bifocals who can adjust, with a swift clap of her hands, the alignment of planets. She scares Hayes, but the children can't get enough of her. They fight over who sits in her lap during the show, and then over who sits on either side of her, in front of her, behind her. "All right, that's enough," she says to a boy who tries to climb up her back. "I am not a monkey bars."

The children, every eight days a new group of children, love this.

"I am the birdman," he tells them.

With Irina in attendance, the children sit still through the entire show, they listen. They volunteer. Hayes places Tara on the shoulder of a sunburned little girl with a single rasta-ribboned braid tucked behind her ear.

"Can anyone tell me where Chick and Tara come from?" he asks.

"Eggs!" a kid guesses.

"Panama!"

"TV!"

"Her claws kind of hurt," the little girl says. "They're digging in."

"That means she's imprinting on you," he says, tapping

the spruce post twice. "She doesn't imprint on everyone." Tara hops off the girl and Chick leans in as if to preen Tara, but Hayes know she's whispering.

"There's a secret word," he tells the children. "And if I say that word, even accidentally, my birds will fly away and leave me forever. What will I do then?"

He doesn't know what he's saying. If Irina weren't there, sitting in the center of the group and nodding solemnly, the children would've wandered off by now.

"You'll cry!" one of the children guesses.

"You'll find a new animal! You'll be the something-else-man!"

"It was a rhetorical question," Hayes says. "Does anyone know what a rhetorical question is?"

No one answers, so either they don't know or they do.

After the show, as he wheels the birds back to their cabin, Irina stops him in the hallway. She places a hand on his arm and says, "Your show, it was so . . . I don't even have a word. Yes I do: lapidary. It was lapidary. I can still feel it, to be honest, in my lap."

"No," Tara says. "No no no no no."

Irina leans in close to the cage, the tendons in her neck quivering and sleek as a frog's thigh. "Is he all right?" Irina asks.

"She," Hayes says. "She's fine. Sometimes she just needs to exercise her, uh, thing."

"Ah," Irina says. "Me too."

"Make it night," Chick says. "Bye now. Bye-bye, hungry lady."

"You'll be getting all superiors on your report."

"All right," Hayes says.

Voice is the word he wants. Sometimes she exercises her voice. He's too distracted by Irina's gravitation and ruddy Dutchness. She makes him feel like he's been caught eavesdropping. She still holds his arm. He feels her hand's heat and his arm's heat producing its own heat, and the feeling is alternately disconcerting and fine.

"We have to go now." Hayes starts wheeling the cage down the hall, whisper-hissing at the birds. "We should do this again sometime."

Back in the cabin, Chick says, "Ned manhandled. Ned bully by her thing."

"I wasn't manhandled." He pushes the cage against the wall and watches the birds watch him. Their expressions, their bodies give no indication of what they're about to say. "I actually felt okay back there. She seems interesting."

"No," Tara says without meeting his eyes. "Not a woman for you. Not a woman."

"Her thing," Chick says again. "Ordure. Virus."

"Okay," Hayes says, unbuttoning his shirt and lying on the bed, "let's shut up now. We've already done our meaningful contact for the day. Let's pretend we're invisible."

"Manhandle," Tara says.

Irina attends their next show, and the next. During the

finale, when the birds fly over the deck, she clasps her hands over her chest like a bereaved peasant. She must know what it means to be abandoned. The possibility exhilarates her, reddens her cheeks. Without her bifocals, which rest atop her head, her face reminds Hayes of a dam-made lake. Liquid, unfocused, hungry, with wildlife buried beneath. He can't stop staring at her.

The birds sigh as they return to their cage. They know, even if Hayes does not, that before Irina he is helpless.

•

Hayes rarely leaves the ship. Where would he go? He'd rather roam the wide, empty decks when the vacationers are gone, visiting the exhibit of ships-in-bottles and the nursery full of babies who have no idea they're on a cruise. Pausing to smile and say hello to the handsome vacuuming hall-maids.

The only port he regularly visits is Tortola, because in Tortola there's a man who will massage Hayes's liver while Hayes lies shirtless on a mat in a dark room. The man says to him, "It is good time. Everyting you say here is highest secret."

He strikes a match and lights a bowl of dried leaves. He claps twice and begins rubbing warm oil into Hayes's stomach.

His hands are conspicuous at first, moving across Hayes's abdomen along his rib cage. Once he starts digging in, though, his hands, or Hayes's awareness of his hands, disappear beneath a churning shroud of sensation.

"I now massage your liver," the man says.

"Okay."

"I continue until you tell me stop."

Hayes closes his eyes and imagines he's being delivered to a butcher. He needs to be stamped with a grade. He's not happy about being cut up for parts, but he enjoys the process. He enjoys it like . . . He once worked for a couple, Betta and Tim, who operated the Farm Animal Reclamation Project. On their hundred acres lived an array of animals rescued from labs and factory farms. Pigs, cows, sheep, rabbits. Hayes was in charge of the rabbits. He fed and watered them, built hutches for new arrivals, named them, talked to them, and, most important, sent photos and personalized letters to each rabbit's adoptive parent.

Hello, I am Huggy, he wrote to Val Downs of Chico, California. *I am an unreluctant rambler. I am always at the head of the pack, kicking out my hind legs in a crazy way!*

Assigning personalities to the rabbits was difficult. Some were exceptional, but most were just kind of rabbity and dull. What could he say? Hello, I am Miss Minnie. I sleep nineteen hours a day! I think I'm depressed! Hello, I am Crackers. I enjoy eating and staring dimly at my fellow bunnies' droppings!

Betta and Tim held hands and toured the grounds, both immensely delighted in overalls. They waved to pigs and cows. At the rabbit enclosure, Tim clasped Hayes's shoulder and said, "Your adoption letters are incredible. Full of tenderness and hard-won insight. It's a gift."

Hayes thanked him, and Betta added, "If animals could talk they'd say exactly what you wrote. They would shame us with devotion."

Betta and Tim walked on to the sheep pen to collect wool and leave it in the woods for birds. Hayes envied their abstract love. It made him want to physically surrender himself to the rabbits, to lie in the center of their enclosure and let them accost him like a salt lick.

One summer, the rabbits began dying. One, two, then three four five at a time. They called veterinarians, tried quarantining the rabbits, changing their diet. By October they had all died. Hayes felt sad and unlucky—he missed them, even the dull, rabbity ones—but Betta and Tim were surprisingly calm. "A farm is a body," Tim said. "When one organ stops working, the body must still endure."

This comforted Hayes for about two hours. It sounded good. But if the farm was a body, and the body lived on, this meant the rabbits were the appendix or tonsils of the farm.

He had forty-seven farewell letters to write. He approached the task solemnly, trying to rid himself of falseness and showmanship. *It's me, Brown Sugar,* he wrote to Ward Yoder of Ogden, Utah. *I have died. I know the world won't be much diminished by my absence. But could you maybe think of me sometime when you cross a field or eat brown sugar? Thanks for adopting me. I loved you.*

He collected what he knew about each rabbit, built the sturdiest nest he could. After a while, he felt tuned to every purr, grunt, and whinny on the farm. He saw secret alliances among the pigs, by how they jostled up and down the trough. Listening to the crows' aggrieved caws, he knew what they were thinking. They were thinking about the missing rabbits.

Here is what Hayes feels while the man in Tortola massages his liver: benign paralysis.

This is what he says: "I am being held hostage by two females. They say they love me. But they don't love me. They love a man named Ned."

"Very high secret," the man says.

"Would you take me home and let me sleep on a mat in your kitchen? You could massage my liver with your foot while you fry eggs."

"The liver," the man says, "when you cut up in tree pieces, it grow into tree new livers. Like starfish."

"That's beautiful." Hayes feels the man's hands again—still—kneading his abdomen. "I hope it's not true." He asks the man to stop and the man does, raising his hands to signal that secret time is over. Hayes offers money, unfolded and organized by denomination. As usual, the man tucks it into the waistband of his shorts. "You pay me much more when we cured," he says.

Hayes repeats it all the way back to the ship, through the market where tourists pollinate the stalls. We cured, we not cured, we cured, we not cured. He buys two cups of diced fruit for the birds. He's pretty sure his liver is permanently damaged.

●

Hayes has run out of stories to tell during meaningful contact. His stories all smolder, spark brush fires, clear forests, leap rivers. The birds see kindling in every word. Their ideal story goes, *Once upon a time, the end.*

They sit in silence until minute eight of meaningful contact. Hayes lies in bed in his underwear, eyes closed, pretending to nap. He sees the birds like slot-machine tabs on the backs of his eyelids. Nothing they say can be trusted, he knows this. Their love is instinctual, impersonal, a mechanism to shield them from harm . . .

"Woman no good," Chick says. "Cruel. Children gather love cruel. Not Ned."

"Ned suckling child," Tara says. "Candy eat boxes of Ned."

Chick is more perceptive than Tara. "Don't go, Ned," she says as he's washing his face. "Don't go," as he pockets his keys and tucks in his shirt. "Don't go." He hears it as he's closing the door and until he's halfway down the hall.

Later, on the sun deck beneath stars pricking dusk into night, Irina takes his hand to make a point about . . . something important that he forgets the moment she takes his hand, and she will not let it go.

Irina says, "You have a way with them."

"Children," Hayes says.

"Birds," she says. "You must train them well."

"I haven't trained them at all," he says. "I think they're the only ones doing the training."

"That won't do," Irina says. Her hand still clutches his. It is like a poultice moistly drawing his polluted humors toward it. "You must come up with rules for these birds, even arbitrary ones. No rules means chaos, looseness, emotion."

Hayes thinks of the Seeing Eye dog with its special patch: DON'T PET ME, I'M WORKING. He studies Irina's warm red face, which seems to be moving closer to his, studies it until they are kissing. It is a long, panicked kiss, filled with movement and refrains and the dull, nauseating whir of the motor, which underlines every quiet moment on the ship. When they're through, Irina steps back and regards him at a distance, shy again. He feels dizzy. He whispers, "The male of the species is superbly equipped."

She apparently doesn't hear him. "No rules equals misunderstanding." They walk around the deck hand in hand. When they've made a complete circuit and have returned to where they kissed, she says, "I will never be lonely again."

"You won't?"

"No no, of course I will," she says. "But right now it doesn't feel like it."

He doesn't want the kiss to be a prelude to anything else. What he wants is for a nature-show voiceover to say, *The male of the species is superbly equipped for these casual comings-together. Watch how happily he walks away. Watch him skipping.* Irina's bifocals rest on the end of her nose and it is dark and her mouth is moist and profoundly ajar. Hayes doesn't want to kiss her again. This first kiss can be its own beginning, middle, and end. It can be a well-stocked larder he can return to again and again in memory.

"Kiss me again," she says.

He kisses her again.

•

It is not love, Hayes is sure, almost sure. It is not sudden, it's not electric. It is not the gossamer convergence of souls. It is not a death scene, a soliloquy, or even a rousing musical number. He doesn't feel pretty, he doesn't feel pretty or witty or bright.

He feels . . . frayed. He can't eat or concentrate or look at himself in the mirror. At night he dreams of Irina lifting, no, tearing away veils and himself saying yes, sure, of course, however, yet, maybe, but.

The birds know. How could they not know? They know. Chick and Tara molt early this year. They preen old feathers from each other's heads, leaving spiked pinfeathers. Hayes dreams of them, too. He's afraid he's going to wake up to the two of them perched on the spare pillow, preparing to peck him blind.

"Ned dry," Tara says during meaningful contact. "Empty time. Run away. Run run away."

"How do you two feel about rules?" Hayes says. "Like, from now on you have to call me Hayes. And: From now on no talking."

"Oh, Ned," Chick says. "When you go away go away. Downtime."

"I'm not going anywhere. I'm the birdman."

"Dogman. Rabbitman," Tara says. "Miceman."

"You want me to tell you a story?"

Both Chick and Tara shift their weight from one leg to the other. Their sharp pinfeathers look like war wear.

"About us," Chick says. "Us about us."

Hayes tells them about when he worked at his old college's psych lab, which tested the effects of maternal deprivation on newborn mice. It turned out that when a newborn mouse is separated from its mother, it goes crazy. It spends most of its time stumbling around, shivering, squealing. He worked nights, cleaning cages and refilling paper-towel dispensers. The students came in, fiddled with the mice, recorded their findings, left. Most of the time they, some five hundred mice and Hayes, were alone.

One night, tired of his job, tired of listening to the plaintive squeaks of motherless mice, he decided to free them. All of them. He found a big cardboard box, loaded them into it, and brought them to a field. He opened the box and turned it onto its side. Some of the mice scurried into the grass, some stayed in the box. Hayes went home pleased.

The head of the lab called him in the next day. He was a big, hairless scientist with furious eyes. He said . . . a lot of things. Hayes was an idiot, the mice were likely already dead, the type of mouse they bought was genetically unsuited to live anywhere but labs. What Hayes remembers clearest was the man staring at his chest, straight through to Hayes's crooked heart, and saying, "You thought you were a shepherd. You're not. You're a monkey governed by one or two petty attachments."

"And you torture mice for a living," Hayes answered. He hoped the scientist would punch him but he didn't. Hayes paid a fine and did some community service. He was too cowardly to ever return to the field, too afraid to find mouse corpses rotting in the high grass.

"Stop, Ned," Chick says. "About us. About us."

"It was just a story. Something that happened to me."

"Five Neds," Tara says. "One Ned five."

"Five times," Chick says.

"You mean I'm your fifth trainer? I don't know what you're trying to say."

Tara says, "Hayes."

"Nigh nigh nigh," Chick says. "Corpse. Corpse shepherd."

"Hayes," Tara says again.

The birds are quiet for the remainder of meaningful

contact, and for the rest of the day, and the next day and so on. Hayes goads them with fruit and new beaded ropes. He makes up rules for the three of them to follow. No more stories about him. From now on during meaningful contact he will read fairy tales, or brochures, the ship's newsletter. No more television after midnight. He tries to calm them by telling them how pretty they are with their fresh feathers. They stare into the mirror hooked onto their cage. They brood.

Irina, on the other hand. She blooms with naked fondness. She has become shyer, hiding her laugh with a hand, seldom mentioning her lap. Hayes has kissed her on each of the six decks and in two unisex bathrooms. When she invites him to her cabin, he always says he has to go take care of Chick and Tara.

"I'm going to be your little bird," she says.

The children who come to their show still jockey to be near her. You, you, you, and you, she says. Chick and Tara fly farther and farther toward open water. They veer and swoop and glide. "What'll I do if they leave me?" he asks the children.

Irina clutches her chest, pledging allegiance.

The birds return with a sigh.

Their shows lately have been remarkable.

•

Hayes is the birdman. Before the birds, he worked with dogs and he was the dogman; before dogs, it was rabbits, and he was the rabbitman; before the rabbits, *mice . . .*

During meaningful contact, while Hayes is reading from the book of fairy tales he checked out of the ship's library, the nonreading part of his brain makes rules.

You should not dress your bird in a showgirl costume. Birds have a whip-sharp sense of decorum, their judgment is crueler, more exact than ours. When you tell your bird *pretty bird pretty bird* ask yourself, Do I mean that *my* bird is a pretty bird? Or am I speaking of a more general ideal pretty bird?

Do not tell your bird you are sorry. Do not mistake need for love.

Look your bird in the eye when you are lying. Scratch your cheek when you are telling the truth.

Hayes is the birdman. He wants, he wants.

Their last show together, Chick and Tara flap their wings before releasing their perch. They fly away with a salutary caw. This is it. Irina stands, shedding children. The birds' outlines become smaller and smaller and smaller and smaller and smaller and smaller. And then they are gone, switched into sky.

Hayes misses them already.

Irina takes his hand and leads him to her cabin.

one dog year

John D. Rockefeller is hungry. On the high dunes, with a nice open view of the ocean, he sits in a wheeled wicker chair, waiting for the airman to arrive. Next to him is Pica, his groom, and below him, a crowd of a few hundred has gathered on the hard-packed sand. The mood is high. Men stand with men and ladies with ladies. Children splash in the shallow water, chasing sandpipers and gulls.

Every so often the crowd grows silent in response to some distant clatter. First, it is a pair of low-slung race cars lurching toward the gathering on the hard sand. When a marching band comes through, the crowd lithely adjusts itself and forms a passageway.

John D watches the ten-man band marching down the beach. Bugles, cornets, drums: happy music, no doubt about it. But its sound is leashed to something easy and sad. Happiness approaching, overtaking, passing him by. John D is eighty-six years old.

Yesterday someone saw him up on the wing, a man is saying. Playing the fiddle. The plane was flying itself.

He sits beneath a diamond-shaped sunshade. His wig is pinned into a straw hat and he wears a collarless shirt, a loose vest made of Japanese paper, and trousers, the pockets filled with dimes. He is no longer the hale viper who was booed by a crowd of women. Who wore tight undergarments to investors' meetings to stay alert. He now measures himself only against himself.

In Florida, he hibernates among palms and oleanders in a gray-shingled house with four dozen casement windows. Two decades earlier, before Cettie died, he forfeited every strand of hair on his body and it never grew back. He resembles an old, scabby seal. He bobs and slips away from worry, the long-standing injuries, the tawdriness, the undiluted stupidity of crowds. He takes potassium bromide for melancholy and bathes off-river in the oxbow lakes of memory. He brightens his own light daily.

He often imagines himself young and on the prow of a ship. Holding on to a mast, steadying himself against the perpetual volatility of the sea, winning, winning . . .

Early on, his father made him draft a list of goals. John D thought of two: Amass one hundred thousand dollars and live for one hundred years. Simple, symmetrical.

You will fail, his father told him. He wanted John D to be a cobbler's apprentice, then a cobbler. A cobbler! To spend perpetuity staring at the soles of shoes.

He is now worth one hundred and eighty million dollars.

His man Pica places a tray over his lap. Pica has been his groom for twenty years. He's seen John D through his most abject days—Tarbell's book, the public backlash, the antitrust proceedings—has dressed him and bathed him and brushed his mangled cuticles with scented emollients. He serves him eight meals a day, always the same: a few steamed crucifers and a glass of fitness juice. Good for the heart, good for the mind. John D is a living-machine.

Enjoyable, John D says after each swallow. But it isn't enjoyable—it is bland fuel. His doctor, who is responsible for the diet, insists he will absorb more nutrients if he takes pleasure in what he eats. And John D wants nutrients. He also wants crab claws, a London broil, chowder, a fried egg, pecan pie.

He scans the beach as he chews, watching the crowd wait for the airman. For the past three days he has been buzzing over town, dropping yellow handbills from his biplane. One of them landed in John D's lap while he was sleeping in his garden. THE ALARMING ACE II WILL PERFORM DEATH-DEFYING FEATS FOR YOUR ENTERTAINMENT. BACK FROM EUROPE AND THE GREAT PLAINS. SEE HIS FAMOUSE DEAD-MAN DROP! ONE DAY ONLY.

Air travel has long interested him, with its steady progression from novelty to verity. Since the handbill landed in his lap, he's dreamed a sky of benign clouds with men and women cutting through. Their arms extended, they call to people on the ground. Come on, come join us. In the dream, John D is on the ground. How awful it is to be on the ground.

In the dream, he thinks that. Awake, though, atop the dune, he is able to turn all he surveys into joy. A woman eating fruit: miraculous. Bicycles: a near-perfect invention. Children: he loves children. Loves their necks and their sluggish awe. Every so often a child approaches his shaded chair, and John D reaches into the pocket of his trousers and pulls out a dime. You have two choices, he says, handing a dime to a ruddy boy. You can save it or you can spend it. What do you think I would advise?

Save it, the boy says.

Of course, of course. You have wonderful throat tendons, do you know that?

I didn't, sir.

And how long do you mean to save this dime? A month, a year?

Until I have as much money as you, sir.

Good boy, John D says. He reaches into his pocket and gives the boy another dime. And is sorry the moment he does it. You have doubled your fortune, he says.

He takes another bite of food while watching the boy retreat. The boy, studying the two winged heads on the dimes, is probably mad at him for the promise he extracted.

John D pushes the plate forward, and Pica, standing behind him, leans in to clear it.

Not yet, he says, taking hold of Pica's sleeve. I want to sit here and enjoy the finishing for a little while. Look, pelicans.

Pica and John D watch a quartet of dust-colored birds fly over the shore. One of the birds stops and plunges into the ocean as if shot. After a few seconds, it ascends with something silver flashing in its mouth.

Hunger, John D says. It rubs out all other urges.

I believe I'm going to start writing down everything you say, Mr. John.

I'm still hungry. Write that down.

Pretty soon I'll have an entire book.

You can take away my plate, John D says. And scratch between my shoulder blades. I have an itch.

While Pica scratches, the old man closes his eyes. Bits of food are caught between his dentures and John D roots them out with his tongue. These are his old dentures, the ones that remind him of twilight and providence's warm paw.

Last year, they were stolen while he slept, during his stay with the governor in a hotel in Miami. The teeth are made of porcelain mounted with gold springs and swivels to twenty-four-karat gold plates. They are exceptional. The plates give liquids a cool, freshwater taste and the porcelain is smooth and shiny. The thief must have reached in between the jalousie slats and grabbed the teeth, soaking in antiseptic on a nightstand, in the middle of the night.

A divine act, he told the governor the next day. The Lord was telling me he can take what he wants *when* he wants. He can pluck it like a berry from a bush.

Please kill me, the governor thought, before I get so greedy for more years. Dump me in the ocean, let the sharks have my organs, let eels nest in my rib cage.

John D tried to be charitable—a man who'd steal another man's teeth must need them for *something*—but after a while he could not help but fantasize about finding the thief and guiding his wrists through a pedal-driven band saw. What use could anyone have possibly made of the teeth? You melt down the gold plates and you have a single cuff link, maybe. A bitty angel charm. The porcelain was worthless. What use, what *use*, he asked Pica.

It was an intimate crime and it left him feeling scornful and inept. The dentist made an exact replica of the old teeth, but they were not the same. They didn't fit right. They made a clicking noise on words like *stop* and *pest*. Food now tasted like . . . food.

He quit wearing teeth around the house. He sat in a wingback rocker, reading inspirational verse and running his tongue along the slick ribbed turtle shell of his palate. What does *numinous* mean? he called to Pica.

Pica looked it up in the dictionary, settled on the fourth entry. Of or relating to numina, he called back.

This did him no good. Without teeth, he felt prepped for the tomb. Every night he and Pica circled around his garden, listening to the distant in-suck of the ocean. It was a sound that reminded John D of blood and his stubborn insides. At the edge of his zinnias, he felt weakened by it. He said to Pica, Could you please carry me. And Pica leaned down and cradled him and lifted him up. He was as light as a bird, scooped out and brittle-boned. Pica carried him through the servants' entrance, up the stairs, to his bedroom.

As Pica was leaving, John D said, Come here. Pica walked over to the bed and John D said, Closer. Pica leaned in and the old man kissed him once, delicately, on the cheek. Thank you, he said.

Then, a few weeks ago, a package arrived. Inside was a set of teeth wrapped in purple crepe paper and a warbly-written note: *Behave or I might steal them again.*

When Pica presented him with the teeth, John D had to blink back tears. Pica washed them in antiseptic and John D put them into his mouth. He smiled, tacked his top molars against his bottom molars, and said, Stop. Pork chop. Pest.

Excuse me? Pica said.

Still clicking. They must have been roughhoused in the mail.

John D touched each tooth with his tongue. Molar, incisor, canine. Welcomed each one back hello, hello, hello. Miraculous, John D said. I'd like you to get me a steamed artichoke, some crab claws, and a glass of fitness juice.

Again John D began wearing the teeth around the house. He wore them during morning tea, during his daily laughing exercises. He even wore them to bed, against doctor's orders. He wasn't worried about choking on one of the gold springs or swivels. These were his *teeth*. He wouldn't allow them out of his sight again, not for a minute.

John D hadn't noticed that when the stolen teeth were returned, the replacement teeth had disappeared. He was too pleased. Pleased with himself, pleased with human-kind. So pleased that he failed to notice that the package had no postmark and the handwriting on the note resembled Pica's, even though Pica had tried to disguise it with his left hand.

The old man felt lucky but diminished. He had been regarding time with the same stubborn miserly purpose with which he regarded money for so many years. But time, contrary to the old saying, is not money. Time is time. It is nontransferable. John D has started wondering what all the straining—the naps, the diet, the laughing exercises—will amount to. What it is worth. A week? A year?

And the teeth? The teeth are a lesson. At times he thinks the lesson is *Life is just.* At other times: *Get prepared.* The old man has been around so long and has touched so many, he cannot help but think he has a shorter conduit to the Almighty. He feels twilight all around him: in flowers wilted on their stems, in mosquitoes telegraphing along porch glass, trying to sketch their way inside, in high clouds, in balloons, in his bones, in the ocean, in shadows, in crowds, and now, especially now, in the constant click-clicking of his new old teeth.

Pica is still scratching. He thinks John D has fallen asleep, and he has. Good boy, Pica says. The old man's wig is slightly off-center. Pica sings one of his secret songs about him. He has about a dozen. This one goes, A mending must come at the ending. But Mr. John's not ready for sending.

He listens to John D's shallow breathing, like a comb through a sandstorm. Seven years left, he sings. Maybe more, maybe less. One dog year in which to protest.

John D's eyes dart open the second Pica takes his hand away.

Has he come and gone? he asks.

Not yet, Pica says. Someone said he often arrives late. To let the anticipation build up. He's a showman.

Were you talking to me while I was asleep?

To be honest, Mr. John, yes I was.

I knew it. Have I told you how I feel about that?

You'd rather I didn't.

No good can come of it. I feel all jumbled now, like I left something behind. Are those boys waving at me?

I believe so, sir.

John D calls to them and the two boys, one skinny, one stout, slowly scale the dune. Neighbor John, the skinny one says. John D, heartened by the young voice, asks the boys a few questions and then hands each a dime. Take care, take extreme care, he says. I want you to invent better ways of doing things.

We will, sir.

You boys are messengers. You are envoys to a time I won't see.

The boys regard him with ebbing enthusiasm. If they linger for a few minutes longer, John D is sure he will extract something useful from them, but he can think of no casual way to hold them. You look like some type of forlorn dog, he says to the stout boy, who acts like he doesn't hear him.

As they leave, the skinny boy drops his dime. Pica, squinting in the sun next to the old man's shaded chair, watches as he falls to his hands and knees to comb through the loose sand. His friend stands by and waits, doesn't even pretend to help search for it.

John D stands up from his chair, extends his elbow to Pica, and together they sidle down the dune. He says, Now where did it go?

Over here, I think, the skinny boy says.

John D and Pica and the two boys prospect through the soft sand. John D closes his eyes, listens to a voice that sounds like his own—a dime is worth more than a dime, it says—reaches his hand into the dune, roots around, and plucks out the coin. It is perhaps the most satisfying thing he has ever done.

I'm sorry, sir, the boy says.

John D hands him the dime and says, Don't waste another day.

A few minutes later, as Pica is straightening the blanket over John D's legs, his doctor and two nurses visit him. The nurses have come to help him with his daily laughing exercises. Laughter, it was recently discovered, prolongs life. John D laughed very little during his working years, so he is trying to gain ground on men who have laughed all their lives.

One of the nurses reads from a book of witty apothegms while the other contorts his face in a variety of ways. The doctor, a young man blurred by politeness, kneels in the sand with his scuffed black instrument bag by his side. There once was a servant, reads the first nurse, who indulged in spending sprees, and who was advised by his master to save against a rainy day. Some time later, the master wanted to know if the servant had amassed any savings. Yes. Indeed I have, sir, the servant said.

Good man, John D interrupts.

The second nurse crosses his eyes and fishes out his lips.

The first nurse hesitates, then reads on, The servant said to his master, But, sir, unfortunately it rained yesterday and now all the money's gone.

John D looks at the second nurse, who has resorted to hitting his palm against his own forehead, and tries to laugh. But he is confused. Why is the money gone? What did the servant spend it on? An umbrella? Did someone steal the money while the servant was drying a wet porch or something and the servant didn't want to tell his master because the master, like some masters, is cruel and the servant, like most servants, is afraid?

The first nurse says, I'm mute.

You don't say, says the second.

John D's laugh comes out heh heh heh. Craggy, mirthless. He laughed so little during his working years because he found so little to laugh about. Every story, true or not, hangs bitter with implication, forward, reverse. Every pill is recalled by an aftertaste.

When the nurses leave, the doctor stands up and reaches beneath John D's crinkled vest to check his heart rate, blood pressure, then his ears, nose, eyes, throat, temperature, joints, scalp, spine, and basal metabolism. John D has promised the man fifty thousand dollars on his, John D's, one hundredth birthday.

The doctor jots illegibly into his notepad. His patient has eczema, bad kidneys, pleurisy. The doctor isn't writing this down. He is making notes for a love letter to another patient, an old woman. *You are the worm in my aorta,* he writes. *You are my delirium tremens.*

John D uses a lever to recline himself in the shaded chair. The high sun turns the white sunshade orange. He says, What ails me today, Doctor? Speak to me, tell me my fortune.

On *speak*, his teeth click.

Only good news, the doctor says. The diet seems to be working. Just look at you, sir. You are the living reward of a life well lived.

I am a prize, aren't I? A living trophy.

Exactly.

Nonsense. All these crucifers. This laughing and fitness juice and hanging on. It's ignoble. I might just fall down dead tomorrow and where would that leave me.

Heaven, the doctor says.

But you aren't a betting man, John D says. Ever since that handbill landed in my lap, I've been dreaming of men with wings. Are men ever born with wings, Doctor?

Sure, the doctor says. And tails and fins, gills. Happens frequently in the Orient. It's all the ocean matter in their diet.

John D sighs. Sometimes it sounds like you don't know a heart from a headstock, he says. It used to be my business to fix other people's faulty connections. I was never the smartest man in the room, or the handsomest or the nicest or the meanest, but I was always the least afraid. What are you writing? Are you drawing a picture of me?

No sir, the doctor says. He writes: *You are a terminal condition. My trough has been poisoned.*

The doctor has quick, pristine hands. John D looks at his own hands: pecked, abraded, danced on by age. He says, I'm no more afraid of dying than of being reborn. Do you know that? Would you kindly look at me when I'm speaking to you?

You are my living end.

The doctor meets his gaze. The old man, fleeced but hardy, looks like some nightmare mascot ready to tunnel to the center of the earth. He looks hungry for a soul.

I am firing you, John D says. You can keep the instruments I bought. Use them on someone else.

The doctor consults his notepad again, as if for a second opinion. Page after page of love notes, of beseeching and woe and heart sauce. He needs a marathon enema and perhaps a vacation in a place where none of the women speak English. He collects his things and zips his bag, brushes the sand from its glossed surface. Is that all? he asks the old man. John D answers, Yes. Until the next thing.

The doctor sidesteps down the dune and nearly bumps into Pica. Aren't you going to stay for the airman? Pica asks him.

There's a woman, another patient, who needs me, he says.

He carries John D's wretched voice with him down the beach. Death, the doctor thinks, is not a thing like birth.

Birth is a dream, spontaneous and innate. Death, on the other hand, is a slow, false, divine calamity. It is like love.

•

An opening, an isthmus between clouds. From above, everything on the ground looks precarious. Tiny lakes and streams blend with foliage until the sun catches them and they shiver and glint like mercury. The swampland resembles an old green floor mat, torn and soaked through in places. Tidy farm plots resemble sewn-on patches. In the ocean, past the crowd waiting on the tan belt of beach, past the downy breakers, monsters rove in shipwreck shadows underwater. The airman is ready.

He arrives low and from the west, towing a heavy rumbling sound that causes the crowd to unanimously turn and raise their chins. John D, immobile on the soft sand, watches the crowd watch the sky. For a moment, he thinks they are saluting him, showing admiration, but they are just using their hands to visor their eyes from the sun. Perhaps he would have given them each a dime, had they been saluting him. But they aren't. They are protecting themselves, awaiting their spectacle. He would have told them to line up and receive their reward. He would have loved that.

The airplane streaks by, dips lower, lower, almost kisses the ocean. Just like the hungry bird. The crowd roars. The airplane arcs and corkscrews back, now moving horizontal to the shoreline. It is a snub-nosed biplane painted gunmetal gray, with two letters on the fuselage: AA II. It flies with impossible grace. It rolls and peaks and buzzes and swerves and herds the crowd like wind herds wheat. It is beautiful, it is irrefutable. It makes John D sleepy.

After a while, he stops tracking the plane altogether and is content to watch the crowd. Gathered together, what are they? They are harnessed parts, a machine manipulated by a smaller, more efficient machine. The input is spectacle, the output is laughter, ecstasy.

Here comes the Dead-man Drop! yells a boy in the crowd.

The engine is silenced and the plane flies vertically downward. At the last moment, the engine chugs back to life and the plane pulls up.

Outstanding, Pica says. He's playing a game with us. To be honest, he reminds me of you, Mr. John. How you were able to outmaneuver whole *systems*. Bypassing and circumventing and pulling up just in time. Leaving us all breathless. Even now, especially now. I bet you're enjoying this, Mr. John.

Yes, John D thinks. He has fallen asleep, though, so he does not reply. Beneath the sunshade, his paper vest blows, a dry bug husk clamped to a branch.

The crowd is nearly insane with admiration for the airman. They are having difficulty finding a suitable way to express it. Husbands kiss their wives, a young girl runs around saying, A toast. A toast. A toast.

Pica reclines John D in his shaded chair. On the brink of

time, when he stands at last, he sings. When his sun has set, and his work is past.

A minute, maybe an hour later, he is awoken by a gentle tugging on his wrist. There is a phrase on his lips, pulled from a muddled dream. As Pica and a young man in a leather helmet come into focus, standing before him, John D utters it: dead-man drop.

The crowd stands below the dune at a respectful distance while the airman gives his regards to John D. The airman is tall and deeply handsome in his airman outfit. Fur collar, denim pants, twenty-eyelet boots. He looks like someone from the future dressed as someone from the past. He gestures with his hands, laughs, pats Pica on the back. The crowd feels his hand on their backs. He is describing his travels to John D, tailoring his story to what he thinks the old man wants to hear. God, beauty, order, magic. The airman is down to his last twenty-five dollars.

Up there, he is saying, you see the real sense and beauty of the world. Everything's touched by God. Dirt is a hundred different shades of brown. Lakes and rivers, they wink at you. Time stretches, shrinks, loses definition—hours pass like seconds, seconds like hours, but all of it, you know, vaccinates you. Is that the right word? Rebaptizes. Years from now, there won't be any reason to stay on the ground. We'll all be kings of the sky.

John D, groggy from his nap, likes the sound of this. He likes the space this man occupies. When the airman asks if he's ever ridden in an airplane, John D nods and answers, No.

Would you like to? And I only ask because some of the main—

Yes, I would, John D interrupts. Pica, please help me up.

And with that, the decision is made. The airman usually has to do more convincing, has to move from the spiritual to the mechanical to convince would-be patrons to fly with him. But John D is awake now. He is not afraid. He stands up from his chair, ducks nimbly around the sunshade to be next to the airman. He clears his throat.

I will now take to the air, he announces to the men and women below the dune. It is something he once heard an acrobat say before a high-wire act. The crowd is subdued, but once they see the old man and the airman and Pica shuffling down the dune, they begin to cheer. John D reaches into his pocket and scatters the rest of his dimes among the crowd like birdseed, not bothering to wait for an outstretched hand.

Pica gently plucks a sandspur from the back of the old man's vest and drops it into the sand. He whispers, It gets real cold up there, Mr. John. The air, he says, isn't as habitual. It's thin. You sure you want to put yourself in jeopardy like this, undo all your hard work? If you want I can go up there for you.

I need you to watch me from down here, John D says. You will wave and I probably won't see you. Make sure everyone else waves as well.

What if there's an accident? Pica says.

Keep waving, John D says.

Down the beach, away from the crowd, the airman pats the airplane's fuselage and says, Hello, Pearl. He opens the latch under the bulkhead and presents the old man with a jacket, helmet, and goggles. Pica helps him remove his wig and replaces it with the helmet. It feels taut and vivified, like a second skin. He is lifted into the cab, latched tight and tucked in with blankets. He is fiercely content: he is on the cusp of something. He moves his legs to make sure they are still there.

Before going through his preflight ritual, the airman hands John D a piece of candy in a wrapper. For your ears, he says. You chew it.

John D opens the wrapper and puts the candy in his mouth. It is powdery, then sweet, then soft. Involuntarily, he chews, his false teeth clicking with every third or fourth bite. It tastes like a peach's secret seed. He continues chewing, resisting the urge to swallow it.

It's made from trees, the airman says. He starts the engine, slips into his shoulder harness, tacks the aileron twice. He plans to take off, bank right, and make an easy, easy circuit over the ocean. No tricks, nothing more complicated than a staggered ascent. He will land on the hard-packed sand and gently ask the millionaire for a contribution. Make a joke about a sky tax. A sky monopoly.

Chewing the gum, John D remembers a day more than

seventy-five years past, when he and his mother took a trip to the doctor. He can't remember why they were there, but he could still envision the brightly colored cuckoo clock in the waiting room and a boy sitting on his mother's lap, greedily licking an amber piece of candy on the end of a small white stick. The doctor kept a jar of them and John D was given one before he left. He saved it until he returned home and then saved it until the following day. He saved it through the next week and through summer and autumn and winter. He saved it until the candy broke into pieces in his bureau drawer. Then he saved the pieces.

You might be the most discreet boy who ever was, his mother used to say.

If he had eaten it, he would have enjoyed it for five minutes. Instead, he enjoyed it for five years.

So went his logic at the time. Now, pinned beneath blankets in the plane, which has begun moving, he wonders what he was saving it for, what squirrel impulse made the idea of eating the candy outrageous. In the cab of the plane, John D feels something like impatience. He chews the gum, which hasn't yet lost its flavor, with more and more fervor.

The plane taxis past and Pica and the rest of the crowd wave. Pica thinks: I will wave until kingdom come. I will be the last thing he sees when his eyes shut for good.

The airman adds and subtracts in his head. The wind has picked up and is blowing the biplane closer to the shoreline. The airplane taxis down the beach, bucking and swaying, and the airman knows he is going to have to tell the old man that they can't risk taking off. For now, he keeps going. From the sound of it, the old man is having a fine time of it.

He is chewing and chewing and chewing, greedily mashing out any patch of sweetness he can find.

It's remarkable. It's the finest thing I have ever tasted, John D says, past the boardwalk, past the dunes, long after it has ceased to be true.

acknowledgments

I'd like to thank the following for their guidance and support: the National Endowment for the Arts; Fred Leebron and Gettysburg College; Eli Horowitz; Ben George; Jordan Bass; Rob Spillman; Christina Thompson; Brandon Heatherstone; my family; my editor, Tim Duggan; PJ Mark; and Corinna, first and dearest reader.